First Edition 2021

Cover Design by Heidi Vilkman
Illustrated by Chris Beaton

Printed in Great Britain by IngramSparks

A CIP catalogue record for this book is available from the British Library

ISBN 978-1-8383871-05

Author's note

The book you hold in your hands is about trees.

On the face of it, it's a romping great adventure about a girl from Ireland and her struggle to find her beloved Uncle Ned.
But the underlying message, subtle but inherent is about the ability of trees to save our world.

Carbon dioxide given off mainly by the burning of coal and gas and the production of meat, is heating up the earth's atmosphere, causing our climate to change. Trees absorb Carbon dioxide and give off oxygen – the air that we breathe, yet we continue to cut them down at a catastrophic rate. *It has never been more important to preserve and protect the trees we have and also to plant millions more.*

More than half the carbon exhaled into the atmosphere by the burning of fossil fuels has been emitted in the last three decades – my adult lifetime. That makes me and and my generation accountable. We cannot assign the task of saving the planet to our children and grandchildren. Each and every one of us can and must do something no matter how small.

I wrote 'Finding Uncle Ned', and *every copy sold will plant a tree.* It is for my grandchildren and children everywhere, for their future.

Finding Uncle Ned

Mary P. Keady

Chapter

I

Ballybay

Uncle Ned didn't look like the type of man who'd be scared of anything. So, as he ran round the house shutting all the windows with a look of sheer terror on his face, I was terrified too. The storm had raged all morning, and I'd watched from my bedroom window as the wind lashed the sea into a frenzy. But for the last few hours, the gentle breeze had barely moved the honeysuckle which climbs up the house and creeps in through my bedroom window.

Now, late afternoon, the wind had started up again, whistling and bouncing off the walls, vibrating the shutters and shaking the house to its very foundations. A raging intruder trying to force its way in. I expected the roof to take off any minute and felt the fear in Uncle Ned as he ran from room to room.

'Go shut the bedroom windows!' he shouted from the kitchen. I raced upstairs and pulled the handle of my bedroom window but couldn't move it. The wind on my face felt warm, blowing in from the Atlantic Ocean, like the gentle Gulf Stream that sometimes buffets the west coast of Ireland.

I put my head out of the window; the force of the wind pulling me forward. The hairs on the back of my neck stood on end, making me tingle all over. Now I didn't feel scared;

quite the opposite. I could hear children's laughter dancing in the breeze. Something or someone was calling my name.

'Jump, Noola! Come on, don't be a scaredy cat, jump.'

I started to laugh as the wind wrapped around me like an invisible blanket. I shut my eyes and imagined fairy-tale castles and riding on unicorns.

But the voices began to fade and became echoes disappearing. I panicked, climbing onto the windowsill and was about to jump off when Uncle Ned grabbed me round the waist and dragged me back into the room, slamming the window shut.

'Jaysus, Noola. Are ye trying to give me a heart attack? Sit there and don't move.'

He ran into the other bedrooms to check the windows were shut, while I sat on my bed, shaken and stunned.

When he came back, his usual ruddy complexion had turned a funny grey colour.

'What's happening, Uncle Ned?' I asked, joining him at the window.

Even though it wasn't yet five o'clock, the sky was dark from the sandstorm swirling in off the beach.

'It's a wuthering wind, the siseesh. I haven't seen the likes of it since I was a boy thirty years ago. There'll be some queer goings-on around here now. There was the last time I saw one of these.'

Uncle Ned got down on his knees so his face was level with mine and put his hands on my shoulders.

'Promise me you'll never do that again. You could have been killed or carried off by the wind. I've heard of loads of people taken by the siseesh: it's dangerous and not to be messed with.'

I nodded but the truth was, I hadn't climbed onto the windowsill of my own accord. Something or someone had made me do it, and I didn't have a clue who or what it was.

I fought the urge to smile because for the first time in my nearly eleven years, I felt truly alive, exhilarated; ready for an adventure. There's no getting away from it: life in Ballybay is dull. When I was little, I'd been content with the daily routine of helping Uncle Ned with his brewing or sitting on the arm of the sofa watching television with Mammy. But now I'm restless – bored. I don't want to spend my days seeing life through a forty-eight-inch screen. So, as I stood, nodding my head with my fingers crossed behind my back, just for a moment, I wished I'd jumped.

Chapter

2

Noola's Boots

On the day after the siseesh, Uncle Ned had gone to the doctor's for his monthly check up.

I wandered into the living room, where Mammy lay stretched out, still in her pyjamas. She was watching a reality TV documentary so I sat on the sofa arm because there was nowhere else to sit.

'What's this about, Mammy?' I asked. She spoke, without looking up.

'It's about lost childhoods, teenagers in prison, and that girl is talking about how she's missing her friends from school. She's written a "bucket list".

'What's a bucket list?' I asked.

'Don't be so simple, Noola. It's a list of things you want to do before you die.'

'But what's that got to do with a bucket? Sure, a bucket's something you put your mop in when you're washing the floor.'

'When you die, they say you've "kicked the bucket", that's what it means. Now shut up, I'm missing the programme with you jabbering on. Go and do something useful. Go make me a brew.'

I stared at the girl on the TV, who for a moment seemed to stare straight back. The TV started to crackle and buzz, and the picture zigzagged and blurred before finally going blank.

Somehow, I knew that was going to happen. I shivered with excitement or fear, maybe both.

'Damn thing,' said Mammy, heaving herself upright and fiddling with the remote. She glared at me as if she knew it was me.

'I thought I told you to make me a brew.'

I disappeared to make the tea, before starting to clean the kitchen so Uncle Ned wouldn't have to do it when he got home. A few minutes later there was a shout from the living room.

'Noola, fetch me a cardigan, will ye? Ned's beggared off without putting the fire on and it's freezing in here.'

I ran upstairs to fetch the cardigan and looked out of the window. The weak, late summer sunshine glistened on the sea, which today was calm and still. I had looked out of that same window thousands of times but today, the view looked different. A fluorescent haze outlined the cliffs, the boulders on the beach, and even the horizon of the sea.

I had to go out and investigate. I ran into the room with the cardigan, then into the kitchen and pulled on my boots just as Mammy shouted again.

'Noola, make me a sandwich, will ye? I'm starving.'

Quietly, I opened the back door. There's no way Mammy would starve, not with all the fat she had wobbling round her belly.

Escaping onto the beach, I ran down to the rock pools. An underwater world of limpets and strange-looking black seaweed covered in little bobbles I liked to pop; a world that bubbled and glimmered and glistened amongst the shadows of the rocks. I touched one of the rocks which shimmered in the curious light like a giant orange jellyfish. A blob of goo stuck to my finger, sending a tingling sensation up my arm, along my shoulders and into my head.

'Weird,' I said, shaking my hand to remove the gloopy substance which plopped into a rock pool, lighting it up like spotlights on a stage. Peering into the shallow water, I saw a hermit crab tugging at some seaweed, trying to release a conch shell. It looked like it'd outgrown its sea snail shell and was looking for a new home. Finding a stick, I eased the conch shell out. The crab stuck its head out of the water and winked at me before pushing the shell into the sand and reversing into it.

I shut my eyes tightly and shook my head. I'm imagining things, I must be - did a crab just wink at me?

I opened them to see two kittiwakes fishing opposite.

Birds never flew away from me when I was on my own, only when I was with Uncle Ned. One of the birds had found a shell and was probing and pecking it, using its bill as a hammer to try to open it.

'I wish I had boots like that pixie girl over there. I could just stamp on these shells. All this pecking is giving me a right headache.'

'Oh, shut up, Seamus, and peck harder.'

I jumped up and staggered backwards, landing with a bump on the sand. I looked around but there was no one there, just me and the two birds… But birds can't talk. I sat motionless for a long time, my heart thundering as I watched the birds struggling with the shells. Picking up a flat rock, I carried it over and put it down in front of them.

'If you hit the shell on this rock, there'll be no resistance so it won't sink into the sand and it'll break much easier.'

To my amazement, the birds started to jump up and down, flapping their wings, and spoke back.

'Well, would ye look at that! The girl's a genius, Bridie. Thank you, pixie girl. Thank you.'

I staggered backwards again, this time tumbling over a large boulder. Peeping round the side of it, I watched the two birds break the shells on the rock one after another. They carried on for half an hour, devouring the grey gooey contents until they were so full, they looked like they wouldn't be able to fly. I watched them warily as they waddled towards me.

'What's your name, pixie girl?' asked the bigger bird. 'I'm Seamus and this is the mother of my eggs, Bridie.'

'Mi name's Fionnuala, but my family call me Noola. You can, too, if you like.'

'Pleased to meet you, Noola. Are you pixie or elf?' asked Bridie.

'Neither, I'm human. I live in the house over there. Come over in the morning and I'll give you the leftovers from breakfast if you like.'

'Well, you're very nice for a human, I must say, but we'd better be away home now. The eggs will be getting cold.'

With that, the birds heaved themselves into the air and flew off. My whole body was trembling, with shock or delight - I couldn't decide which. I skipped across the beach towards the caves, feeling happy this morning, carefree even.

The Echo Caves are nestled at the bottom of a steep curve of limestone rock, carved out thousands of years ago by the sea. The caves had been nicknamed "Echo Caves" by the locals because when you speak, your voice bounces off the walls and speaks back to you. They're spooky and I only ever go in them with Uncle Ned. But today, as I dipped my head under the canopy of rock that hung over the entrance, I didn't feel afraid.

'Hawarye!' I shouted as I entered the dimly lit caves.

'Warye warye warye,' the caves echoed back.

'Cor blimey, what's a fella supposed to do to get a decent night's sleep around here?'

I looked around to see where the voice was coming from, but there was no one in sight.

I shouted again.

'Hawarye!'

'Warye warye warye,' my voice echoed back.

'Scuse me, missy. D'ya mind buttoning it?' came a voice from above.

'Aw, you button it, Wombat! Can't ye see she's just a little girl?'

I looked up and squinted into the darkness. There, hanging from the roof, were two huge bats; they must have been at least a metre long. I shut my eyes tight for a few moments before opening them again. The bats were still there. I told myself I must be seeing things… maybe…probably, but five minutes ago… I had just been talking to two seagulls.

'Am I seeing things or are there two gigantic bats up there?' I asked.

'Yes, there is. I mean, there are, and we're trying to sleep,' said one of them. My mouth went dry and I stood perfectly still, afraid to blink in case they disappeared. My heart wasn't still though it was threatening to burst through my chest.

'Oh, s-s-sorry, I didn't think there was anyone here. I'm sorry if I woke yous,' I said, edging away from them.

'Aw, take no notice of him. He's always grumpy if he hasn't had enough sleep. I'm Dingbat and me grumpy mate here's Wombat. Pleased to meet ya, little girl.'

I backed away a few paces, holding onto the wall and tracing my steps towards the cave entrance. The bats seemed friendly enough but I didn't want to get too close.

'I'm Noola O'Brien. Pleased to meet you, too. I didn't know bats lived in here.'

'We don't live here. We flew in from Africa on the siseesh, but we're originally from Australia. We aren't stopping round here, though. It's too cold. We're heading south - somewhere warmer.'

'Why don't you go to America? My Uncle Ned's going to take me one day. He says it's nice there.'

'Nah… the bats there eat insects, not fruit… Don't like insects; nasty creepy crawly things,' said Dingbat.

'Well, why didn't you stay in Australia?' I said.

'They chopped our tree down to make way for a new town, so we had nowhere to live. That's the trouble with humans, they're always meddling. They bulldozed half our forest, then the rest was torched by slash-and-burn farmers, and when the farmers aren't burning the forests, the sun does the job for them. If we hadn't left, we'd have ended up roasted alive.'

I tried to imagine what a slash-and-burn farmer would look like. The farmers in Ballybay are big and jolly with red faces. I couldn't imagine them as knife-wielding arsonists.

I changed the subject.

'Do bats live in caves in Australia?'

'No, we live in trees and eat fruit. That's why we're called "fruit bats", ye dummy,' said Wombat. 'Caves are nasty smelly places and I, for one, can't wait to get out of here. We jumped off the siseesh early to do a bit of sightseeing. Wish we'd stayed on it now.'

'Why didn't you stay in Africa?' I asked. 'It's warm there.'

'Africa's as bad as Australia. They chop down the trees for mining, and besides, we couldn't get to grips with the language,' said Dingbat.

'Well, if you'd stayed on the siseesh, where would it have taken you?' Dingbat scratched his nose with his wing.

'To the Otherworld, but we don't wanna live with a bunch of fairies.'

I was about to ask where the Otherworld was when Wombat interrupted.

'Look, missy, I don't want to be rude, but would ya stop asking questions. We've got a long journey ahead of us and I really need to get some shut-eye.'

'Oh, I'm sorry. I'll be away home now. Good luck. I hope you find somewhere nice and warm to live.'

'Nice to meet you, Noola O'Brien. You take care now,' said Dingbat.

I left the caves and leaned against the cool rocky outcrop. The waves crashing onto the shore, echoed the pounding in my chest. Uncle Ned had said there'd be strange goings-on after the siseesh. It had to be that; what else could it be?

I skipped home, singing all the way and feeling like a giant balloon was floating inside me. I had just been talking to some seagulls, and some fruit bats! I couldn't wait to tell Uncle Ned.

I found him making soda bread in the kitchen. 'Uncle Ned, I've made some friends at last! I've been talking to Bridie and Seamus, they're kittiwakes, and Dingbat and Wombat, they're fruit bats, they were in the echo caves.

Uncle Ned raised an eyebrow.

'Fruit bats!' he said, looking shocked.

'Well, would ye believe it. I told you there'd be strange goings-on after the siseesh.'

'They've come from Africa. I'm going back out to see if I can find anyone else to talk to.'

On my way out, I heard a door slam. Uncle Ned was in the living room arguing with Mammy so I stretched up to the window to see what was happening.

'Bridget, this has gone too far. Noola needs some friends. She's had to resort to talking to the seagulls… and,' he said, scratching his head, 'fruit bats!'

Mammy jumped up. Her eyes grew wide and for a moment I could have sworn she looked frightened.

'See, I told you she was simple,' she said.

'She's not simple she's lonely, and come September I'm enrolling her for school, whether you like it or not,' said Uncle Ned. The door slammed, and he went back into the kitchen as Mammy shouted again, but this time at the closed door.

'Noola can't go. The bullies will have a field day. Believe me, I should know.'

I wondered what she meant.

Mammy sat back and finished off the remainder of her crisps. and I watched her screw up the packet and launch it at the wastepaper basket. She missed.

'She's not going and that's final,' she said, plumping up the cushions and settling herself back down.

Chapter

3

Ned O'Brien

The following day, I woke early after a restless night dreaming about talking seagulls and bats.

A cool breeze blew in from the Atlantic Ocean and sinister-looking sea mists swirled across the beach and the surrounding dells and glens.

As I looked out of my bedroom window, I half expected a pirate ship to appear out of the mists; since the siseesh, and the events of yesterday, anything seemed possible.

It was Friday and that meant fish for tea. In Ireland we still followed the old rules of the Catholic Church, which meant no meat on a Friday.

'Noola, are ye coming down to the beach to see Jimmy? He'll be back with his catch and I've got a couple of bottles for him,' shouted Uncle Ned. I ran downstairs, pulled on my boots and looked outside for Bridie and Seamus, but they were nowhere in sight.

We set off down the shingle path to the beach. It was still breezy and the crashing waves disappearing out to sea looked like someone had poured bubble bath on them, but the sand was soft and flat. Uncle Ned found a big stick and wrote in the sand, "Fionnuala Isabel Maddison Rose O'Brien," and then his name, "Ned".

'How come my name's got hundreds of letters Uncle Ned, and yours only has a few?' I asked.

'Well, my little pixie princess, Fionnuala and Isabel are your grandmothers' names and Maddison Rose, well, I think your mammy got them names from one of those soap operas she's always watching. My mammy never had a telly so I'm just plain old Ned.'

He lifted me onto his shoulders and I laughed as we galloped across the beach towards the sea.

Out in the bay, a few anchored fishing boats were being tossed about in the choppy water. In the distance, the waves rolled and broke against the beach where Jimmy Joyce was unloading the catch from his boat, a traditional Irish hooker, built for fishing in the shallow waters of the bay.

I stood on a lobster cage and climbed up to look over the side. The clouds parted and a shaft of light shone through them.

'Look, Uncle Ned. It's God's rays shining on the fishes!' I shouted.

The sunlight made the fish sparkle like jewels, iridescent in the morning sunshine. Some of the fish were still moving: the sudden flick of a tail, a mouth opening and closing - small clues of creatures clinging to life.

I could hear them murmuring,

'Help us, save us.'

I watched them as if in a trance, and hundreds of small black beetle-like eyes stared back at me. I jumped down from the boat.

'Uncle Ned, can you hear the fishes?' I whispered.

Uncle Ned wrinkled his nose and laughed.

'No, but I sure can smell them.' The skin on my arms began to prickle and I decided I was never going to eat fish again.

'Hawarye, Red?' shouted Jimmy. 'Have ye got me bottles?'

Uncle Ned reached into his jacket and pulled two bottles from his inside pocket.

'Sure, I have that Jimmy, and it's a great batch. It'll put hairs on yer chest, sure it will. It's got the kick of a mule,' he said, passing them to him.

'Take as many fishes as ye want. There's herring and a few mackerel,' said Jimmy.

I watched Uncle Ned as he leaned easily over the boat to get the fish. He seemed like a giant to me; six foot six inches without his shoes.

My daddy told me that Uncle Ned had been nicknamed "Red" by his friends when he was young because of his wild mane of red hair. Later, he'd grown a bushy red beard as well. When I asked him why his face was so red, he said that years of living by the sea had made him weather-beaten, and his habit of drinking home-made whiskey every day had given him a bright red nose. I watched him fill the bag, the fish now still and quiet and realised that "Red" was a very appropriate nickname for Uncle Ned.

'Look, Noola, it's the dolphins from Dingle,' shouted Jimmy, pointing at two dolphins frolicking near the shore.

I ran to the edge of the water and watched the dolphins blowing bubbles and performing cartwheels in the current, climbing the frothy foam and disappearing under and over each other.

'They're putting on a show for you, Noola,' said Uncle Ned, appearing next to me. Jimmy joined us, throwing them some fish and causing them to jump even higher. Uncle Ned whistled as I jumped up and down, clapping my hands.

The dolphins whistled back, flapping their fins together, mimicking our applause. I laughed and closed my eyes tightly to capture the memory for ever. I opened them as the dolphins did one last somersault before disappearing out to sea. We carried on cheering and clapping until they were out of sight.

'See ye same time next week,' shouted Jimmy, heading back to his boat.

'Sure will,' said Uncle Ned, still smiling. 'Come on, let's go get some breakfast.'

As we walked back up the shingle path towards the house, Uncle Ned stopped to look at it.

'Sure, I'll have to get a proper roof put on the house before winter sets in. It's starting to leak like a sieve.'

'How come it hasn't got a proper roof, Uncle Ned?' I asked.

'My daddy built that house, but he died before he got round to finishing it. Me and your daddy, we were only kids.'

I tried to imagine Daddy and Uncle Ned as kids. Even though Daddy's the oldest, he's much smaller. His image in my mind is blurry, probably because he hardly comes home anymore.

'Why didn't Mammy and Daddy get their own house?' I asked.

'Sure, what's the point of me rattling round in that big old house on my own?.

I told them so, but I think your mammy had already realised that if she got her own house, she'd have to clean it. And she wouldn't have a ready-made babysitter.'

I looked at the house. A grey square, surrounded by grey boulders, under a grey sky.

'It looks like a box dropped from the sky onto the moon,' I said, turning round to look at the only other house in the bay.

'Now the cottage, that looks like one of those houses you see on the boxes of fudge in Murphy's. It's really pretty even though it's empty and run down.'

Uncle Ned nodded.

'I bet the roof on that doesn't leak; they built them properly in them days. I'll have to get your daddy to help me fix our roof when he comes home. He should be back in a couple of days.'

I know that Daddy won't stay long and I don't really care. It used to make me sad, but now he's just a picture on the sideboard and a stranger that comes to visit once in a while.

We climbed the steep steps to the house and walked through the paved yard, and past the shed and raised beds where Uncle Ned grows potatoes. Out of these, he makes moonshine - an illegal whiskey - for himself and the locals.

As we reached the house, he looked out to sea.

'Ye know, on a clear day ye can see America from this very spot. One day,' he said, 'we'll go to New York and we'll go down to Rhode Island to see the shrimp boats come in. I've heard they have the best shrimps in the world there.'

'Hey, Ned. Fetch me a cup of tea, will ye? I'm parched,' shouted Mammy from the living room.

Uncle Ned shut the kitchen door.

'She can lift her lazy backside off the sofa and get it herself.'

I filled the kettle and placed it on the stove.

'I'll make the tea,' I said. 'If she has to get up and leave the television there'll be a massive row, and you've already said that the doctor told you to take it easy when you saw him last week.'

The back door opened and Jon Connolly, Con to his friends, shuffled into the kitchen, throwing his flat cap onto the table. He smiled a wrinkled, toothless smile at me and winked.

'Bout ya, Red. Noola, hawarye?' he said, leaning on the table.

'I'm good,' I said, rummaging in the cupboard for the breakfast cereal, while Uncle Ned reached up to the top shelf where he kept the whiskey.

'I'm grand at the moment, Con. Would ye be after having a drop o' the old moonshine?' he said, getting out the glasses.

'Ah, go on then. I may as well try a drop while I'm here,' said Con.

I quickly moved Mammy's latest magazine subscription off the chair as Con tottered towards it. He leaned against it, panting and grinning before lowering himself into it and crossing his bony legs.

'Sure, that was a rare storm the other day,' he said. 'They're all talking about it in Ballybay. Nelly Noonan swears she's seen pixies, and that can only mean one thing - trouble and mischief.'

Uncle Ned frowned at Con, then arched his eyebrows while nodding his head towards me. It's his code for, 'Don't say things like that in front of Noola.'

Con looked sideways at me and lowered his head.

'Sure, I'm just after coming from the post office where I was talking to Gerry Doyle. He told me that a family from Cork are after having that place across the bay and turning it into a holiday cottage. Sure, I thought I'd come and fill yis in.'

'Well, would ya believe it? That place looks like it's not fit to keep pigs in,' said Uncle Ned, handing Con a glass of whiskey.

'And some hoity-toities arrive, thinking they're posh and all that, and turning it into a holiday cottage.'

'Would they be having any kids and all that?' I asked. Maybe I'd have someone to play with during the holidays.

'Two wee boys, from what I hear,' said Con. 'One about your age and the other a bit younger. They're strange folk from the south, not right friendly, but happen the kids might be different. Ye never know.'

I looked out of the window and my heart did a secret cartwheel. Searching for crabs and climbing the rocks would be twice as much fun if I had someone to play with.

Con finished his whiskey and shuffled out of the house. He got on his pushbike and I watched him as he disappeared down the winding coast road towards Ballybay.

'Don't you think it's weird that Con, who can hardly walk, manages to cycle from Ballybay and back every day, Uncle Ned?' Uncle Ned was washing the glasses in the sink. He turned round and smiled.

'It's amazing what people will do for a glass of my whiskey.'

'Well why doesn't he take some home, then he wouldn't have to pedal here every day? That would make more sense to me.'

'He's a good friend, and ye know he loves to be out and about spreading the local gossip. He's making the best of what time he's got left, because ye never know what's round the corner. Like me old ma used to say, destiny's like an old coat. Ye can't change it, ye just make it fit the best ye can.'

I sat looking out of the window, imagining what it would be like to have a friend, someone to climb the rocks and collect shells with, or go into town and have a can of cola in Murphy's, and maybe even spend a few euros on the slot machines. I was still daydreaming when Mammy came into the kitchen. I'd forgotten to make her tea and she didn't look happy.

'Bridget,' said Uncle Ned, 'I've been looking into it and the school bus comes to the crossroads down by the old cottage. Noola's old enough now to catch it on her own.' Mammy poured herself a cup of tea and started to make herself a huge cheese sandwich. She scowled at Uncle Ned, her face drawn downwards.

'Sure, you're doing a fine job home-schooling her, and besides, the bus fares would cost a fortune. And then she would have to have her dinner. And then there's the uniform and the school trips – the list goes on and on.' She bit her sandwich and carried on speaking as she chewed.

'Schooling never did me any good and look at me now. I don't have to work. When she's old enough, she needs to find a good man to look after her, like I did. Besides,' Mammy's voice dropped to a whisper,

'what about those ears, for God's sake? We'd be the laughingstock of Ballybay within a week.'

I caught sight of myself in the cracked mirror on the back of the kitchen door. My hair doesn't fall softly on to my shoulders like the girls in Mammy's catalogue. It's wiry like the pan scrubbers Uncle Ned uses for doing the dishes; it's the colour of carrots and sticks out at right angles from the sides of my head like orange candyfloss. My nose is too small for my face, which is covered in freckles and always looks like it needs washing, but worst of all, my ears are pointed like the man off Star Trek and they stick out through my frizzy ginger hair. I could tell by the look on Uncle Ned's face he was raging but arguing with Mammy is pointless. She always gets her own way.

'Catch yourself on, Bridget. Sure, Noola needs to go to school. I can only teach her so much. Not everyone wants to lay about watching TV all day. Some people want to do something meaningful with their lives.'

I joined in.

'Please, Mammy. If I can go to school, I'll be able to get a good job and help with the housekeeping and all that,' I said.

Mammy's face was set like a statue.

'You're not going and that's final,' she said, wandering back into the living room, still in her pyjamas.

I went upstairs, got a pen and my notebook out of my drawer and threw myself onto my bed. I started to write a bucket list.

Chapter

4

The Boys from Cork

Uncle Ned had been to the hospital and brought back
a big box of books from a junk shop in Galway.
'What's this one about, Uncle Ned?' I asked, pulling
one out.

'It's called Irish Myths and Legends. Here, I'll read it to ye,'
he said, sitting down at the kitchen table. He cleared his throat.

'The Otherworld is a magical place that exists close to ours
and overlaps from time to time and place to place. Enchanted
forests, fairy hills and mystical caves are all known to be
entrances to another world. A world where fairies, elves,
pixies, goblins and dwarfs live happily amongst the wild
spirits of nature, a place that can only be reached by those
who are touched by fairy magic.'

'Have you ever seen a fairy, Uncle Ned?' I asked, as he
paused to take a drink of his tea.'

'Of course, I have,' he winked. But ye know those creatures
are not for the eyes of mere mortals.'

I was about to ask what a meremortal was when Uncle
Ned dropped the book and started to make strange rasping
noises. The same noise I'd heard from a seagull choking on an
extra-large mackerel.

I watched in alarm as he clutched his chest and turned a
funny grey colour.

I rushed to the kitchen cupboard to find an aspirin and pour him a glass of water.

'Are you alright, Uncle Ned?' I asked as he sipped the water and slowly regained his normal colour.

'Don't be fretting over me, Noola. I'm fine,' he said, sitting down in his usual chair by the stove. I picked up the book to finish the story as the sound of children's laughter drifted through the kitchen window. I jumped up and ran to the door.

'Kids, Uncle Ned! It's some kids to play with.'

Two small boys were skipping down the shingle path to the beach. They both had sticks with tin cans attached to them; they looked like they were going fishing. Uncle Ned followed me to the door and smiled.

'Jaysus, would ye look at that! It's the two boys from the holiday cottage. Go on, say hello.'

I pulled on my boots and ran after the boys, catching them up just as they reached the rock pools and were dangling their tins in the water.

'Hawarye? I'm Noola O'Brien. I live in the house over there.' The boys looked up. They were identical, with the same curly brown hair and startling blue eyes, but one of them was quite a lot smaller than the other.

'Look, Sean. it's an alien from outer space,' said the little one.

'Don't be daft, Fintan. That's not an alien, it's one of them there changelings that Mammy was telling us about. Sure, there's loads around these parts,' said the bigger boy, picking up a handful of pebbles from the rock pools and throwing them at me.

'Away wit ye, ye weirdo. We don't play wit your sort,' he shouted, picking up another handful. The smaller boy copied his brother and the stones rained down on me, stinging me all over.

I stood still, my stomach contracting as if a giant hand was squeezing it. Tears filled my eyes and I turned and ran back up the shingle path, my face burning with the shame of it. Hot salty tears trickled down my face; soon they were dripping off my nose. I slammed the gate, startling Bridie and Seamus who were hopping up and down, waiting for their breakfast. I ran inside where Uncle Ned dozed in the chair by the fire and pulled out yesterday's soda bread. Uncle Ned made a fresh loaf every day. I broke it into bits, ran out, and fed it to the hungry birds.

After they had eaten every last crumb, Seamus asked,

'Are you coming down to the rock pools with us?'

I watched the two boys climbing the rocks which rose steeply on either side of the bay, my eyes still blurry with tears. I stared at my boots and tried to keep the anger out of my voice.

'No, I have to help my Uncle Ned, but you two need to get back to your eggs. I just heard those two boys talking and they said they were going looking for birds' eggs, and when they find them, they're going to smash them onto the rocks.'

The birds flew off towards the boys. Swooping down on them, their wings battered the boys' heads, and their talons clawed their faces. The boys screamed and begged them to stop, but the birds carried on as the boys clambered down the rocks and ran home.

My heart felt like a rock in my chest and I knew I shouldn't have done that. As I walked down the path towards the beach, the cold wind stung my cheeks and I had never felt so lonely in my whole life.

Chapter

5

The Changelings

That evening after supper, I was sitting in the kitchen in front of the fire with Uncle Ned. He was drinking a glass of whiskey while I was having a cup of hot chocolate before I went to bed.

'Uncle Ned, what's a changeling?' Those boys from Cork wouldn't let me play with them. They said I was a changeling and that there's loads of them round here.'

Uncle Ned looked at me, his eyes darkened and I could tell he was raging.

'Sure, take no notice of those eejits. You're not a changeling. Sure, I saw you straight after you were born. You had the same little frizzlebob hair and the same little pixie ears as you have now. I should have told you about the changelings before but I didn't want to frighten you.' He settled back in his chair and carried on.

'You know how I told you about the Otherworld, how it's real and not just in fairy stories?' he said. I nodded and sat down on the rug in front of him.

'Well, there are some places in this world that are so magical and at one with nature - and Ballybay is one of them places - that the veil between our world and the Otherworld is thin and creatures from there cross over. When the siseesh came, it brought creatures from the Otherworld.' I looked up at Uncle Ned and from the look on his face, I knew he wasn't making this up.

'What exactly is a siseesh, Uncle Ned?' I asked.

'When the wind starts up in an enchanted forest, something happens: the natural and the supernatural collide. The force of nature combines with the mystical force of fairy sprites, and a siseesh begins. It travels the lands, picking up those with fairy blood. It's very powerful. The creatures it picks up are not always good. There's good ones and bad ones, just like there's good and bad people, and this time it brought a band of Spriggan Elves. They're over in Gilligan's Glen.'

I shuffled nearer to the fire, hugging my hot chocolate to my chest.

'Now the Spriggans are a travelling band of villains. They're destructive and dangerous. They steal human babies and put one of their own in its place. They only take the most beautiful, fair-haired babies to inject their weak stock with a healthy human strain.' Uncle Ned leaned back in his chair and took another sip of whiskey, as shadows from the firelight flickered across his face.

'The child they leave is hideous. This child is called a changeling, and it's true, there are quite a few of them round here now.'

'But that's terrible, Uncle Ned. Is it true? Have you ever seen any of these changelings?' I asked, as goosebumps crept up my arms and prickled the back of my neck.

'As sure as I'm sat here it is. Sam Kelly's son, Teddy, was taken. He had blond curly hair and a beautiful chubby face with red, rosy cheeks. Sure, the child they left in his place has eyes and hair as black as coal. They say he'll only eat raw meat.' I swallowed hard. I'd never be able to look in the window of Dooley's butchers in Ballybay again.

Uncle Ned took another sip of his whiskey and carried on.

'Anyway, Sam wants to put him on a shovel and put him on the fire because if it's a true changeling, legend says it will fly up the chimney and the real baby will appear on the doorstep, but his wife Sarah won't let him. She says any child is a child of God and she won't murder it. Child of God it never is – child of the devil, more like.'

I shivered. 'Do you know any more changelings, Uncle Ned?'

'Biddy O'Dowd's granddaughter, Niamh, was taken. She had the same blonde curly hair and the sweetest face with little rosebud lips. She was as pretty as a picture.

'Niamh's mother won't have anything to do with the creature they left in her place so Biddy has to look after her. She takes her to church every day, hoping for a miracle. I'd fight any man in Ireland with me bare fists, sure I would, even though I've got a dodgy ticker, but when I saw Biddy in Ballybay and stuck my head in the pram, I nearly passed out with shock. The child was so shrunken and wizened it scared the pants off me.'

'If changelings are so ugly, why did those boys say I was one? Am I as ugly as those changelings, Uncle Ned?'

'No, my darling, you're not ugly, but you're different, and kids don't like other kids that are different. They like to fit in. You come from a long line of,' Uncle Ned scratched his beard and sighed. 'Well, let's just say your family's very unusual, to say the least. Anyhow, that's enough of all this talk. Get off to bed and I'll come and say goodnight in a little while.'

I lay in bed trying to push the images of the changelings out of my head. Eventually I fell asleep and had a strange dream. In the dream there was a very tall woman with long grey hair, wearing a purple and blue cloak. She had hold of my hand and was leading me somewhere. We were in a wood but not a dark, dreary one. It was bright and warm, with huge colourful butterflies and giant bees flying around. I had never seen anywhere like it, apart from in the books that Uncle Ned brought home. Under one of the trees were some flowering

plants. I noticed them because they were so bright. The leaves were so dark they were almost black, in contrast to the hot pink flowers which looked good enough to eat. I bent down and picked one. It felt sticky. I put it in my mouth, watching the woman in the cloak to see her reaction but the woman was talking to a tree. I felt an explosion of sweetness, then the strange sensation of popping candy, and with the popping I woke up.

I lay in the darkness, rubbing the sleep out of my eyes and looked out at the moon. My fingers were sticky so I licked them. They tasted sweet and smelled of flowers. I nestled my head into the pillow, trying to remember the face of the woman in the cloak. As I drifted off to sleep, a slight breeze blew through my half - open window, barely moving the curtains as it passed.

Chapter

6

An Unforgettable Birthday

I t was the end of August. The boys from Cork had gone home, and a FOR SALE sign had gone up in the garden of the holiday cottage.

Today was my eleventh birthday.

I woke up to find a small box on my dressing table, tied up with a bright red ribbon. Normally, I would get colouring books and pencils. But this looked like something much more interesting. I opened the parcel to find a St Christopher medallion. It was Uncle Ned's, handed down to him through three generations. I ran downstairs to find him.

'I love it Uncle Ned, but it's yours.'

'Not anymore. It's yours - to keep you safe,' he said.

'But who's going to keep you safe now?' I said.

'Oh, don't worry about me. I'll be around for a little while longer, I hope. Happy birthday! Here, I'll put it on for ye.'

Uncle Ned fastened the necklace round my neck and a rush of warmth pulsed through me, as if it was protecting me already.

'There you go,' he said, smiling. His voice sounded soft, almost sad.

'I want you to know that even when I'm not around, I'm still with you. I'll always be with you. And one day, when you have to stand on your own two feet and be strong, this medallion will help you.'

'Uncle Ned, please don't say things like that,' I said, turning away as tears filled my eyes. The thought of a world without him was terrifying. I held the medallion up to look at it closely. Engraved into it was a man carrying a young child on his shoulders. As I examined it, Mammy came into the kitchen.

'What's that you've got there?' she asked. I wiped my eyes with my sleeve and held the St Christopher up for her to see.

'Oh, it's your birthday, isn't it? I'll take you into Ballybay sometime and buy you a new coat,' she said, rifling through the cupboard to find the cornflakes. I rarely got new clothes; most of my clothes came from my cousin in Dublin, who is two years older. I get a parcel when Daddy calls off on his way home from England. He's due home any day now. Maybe there'll be a coat in the parcel. The one I have is still too long.

'Thanks, Mammy,' I said, trying to sound pleased. I knew Mammy would never take me into Ballybay, never mind buy me a new coat. She went back to the TV as I opened a card from Daddy. At least he'd remembered. As I read it, I noticed that the handwriting looked surprisingly similar to Uncle Ned's. Maybe Daddy hadn't remembered after all.

'What're you looking at Uncle Ned?' I asked, as I watched him staring out of the window, a faraway look on his face.

'I had a strange dream last night. I dreamt I was being carried away by the wind. It seemed so real, and you know when you wake up but you're still half asleep and you're still dreaming and you don't want the dream to end, it felt like that. It was nice.' He turned round and shook his head as if shaking the thoughts away.

'Come on, let's make today a special day.'

It was a fine day, but breezy.

'Kites,' he said, rummaging through the cupboard and finding an old magazine with some kite-making instructions. That's what we should do on a day like this - fly kites.

Uncle Ned set off to find some things to make the kites. He came back with some wood, some tape, some string, a bin liner and some scissors.

'Go and find some ribbons Noola, to make them look pretty and all that.'

When I got back, Uncle Ned had cleared the kitchen table and started to make the kites. After about an hour, they were finished and we set off to the beach. The wind hummed and the kites flew magnificently, hovering and swooping like young sea hawks.

As I ran towards the sea, my kite was flying higher and higher. I looked up to see Uncle Ned's flying past mine and out to sea.

'Uncle Ned, you've let it go!' I shouted and turned round to see him lying motionless on the sand.

I watched as the kite soared skywards, like a soul released from its earthly body. Flying towards heaven and eternity, the yellow ribbons flailing behind it, the last tenuous link between this world and the next.

I let go of my kite and it flew out to sea.

I ran towards Uncle Ned, a quiet moan rising in my throat turned into a silent scream. I could hear the waves crashing onto the beach and the distant clamour of gulls nesting on the cliffs.

Everything was happening in slow motion and my legs turned to rubber as I staggered towards Uncle Ned, still motionless on the sand. His eyes were shut as if he was asleep so I started to shake him.

'Wake up, Uncle Ned. Please,…please, wake up,' I said, as tears tumbled down my cheeks.

After what seemed like hours but could only have been a few minutes, I gave up. I lay down next to him, hoping he knew I was there. I knew I'd never be able to get him home and the tide was coming in, so I closed my eyes.

A numbness entered my body and I grew terribly cold. All I could hear was the sound of the sea and my heart beating.

I woke up the day after. The early morning light seeped into my room through a slit in the curtains, lighting up Daddy's face. He was sat at the side of my bed, his eyes red from crying, and I realised it hadn't all been a terrible dream.

'Hi, Noola,' he said, wringing his hands.

'Where's, Uncle Ned?' I asked. Daddy looked out of the window and rubbed his eyes.

'Jimmy brought you home,' he said. 'He got back with his catch and heard two seagulls. They were pulling at your clothes. He thought they were attacking you. The tide was coming in fast. It had covered your feet so he picked you up and carried you home.'

'That'd be Bridie and Seamus,' I said quietly. Daddy looked at me baffled.

'Who?'

'Where's Uncle Ned?' I asked again, trying to sit up. My body wouldn't move, paralysed with fear.

Daddy carried on looking out of the window.

'The funny thing is, the gulls followed him. He left you in the garden because the door was locked and he ran back for Ned. Your mammy said she only found you because the gulls were making an awful racket and pecking at the window.'

'Where is he?' I asked again, my voice barely a whisper.

Daddy's eyes misted over and tears spilled down his face, filling me with terror.

'When Jimmy got back to the beach… Ned was gone.'

Chapter

7

The Wake

The next few days passed by in a blur. Uncle Ned hadn't been found and I was happy about that. He'd always wanted to cross the Atlantic Ocean to America, and now when I thought of him, he was swimming to New York to see the Statue of Liberty.

For two days I stayed in bed, but on the third day I heard loud chattering coming from downstairs. I peered round the banister. The door to the kitchen was open wide enough to see a crowd of people.

Daddy was sat on the stairs, his elbows on his knees, his head cupped in his hands. I sat down beside him and he looked up. His mouth smiled but his eyes told a different story.

'Hawarye, Noola?' he asked.

'Have they found him?' I said, looking down at the people in the room.

Daddy hung his head.

'Not yet.'

We sat in silence, listening to the postman, Gerry Doyle.

'Sure, it was a short life, but a life well lived. Ned O'Brien knew how to enjoy himself.' There was clink of glasses and Con joined the banter.

'Here's to you, Ned. Sure, he'd be having one himself if he was with us.' My nails dug deep into the palms of my hands.

Daddy sighed and put his arm round my shoulders.

'Everyone's come from miles around; they've all got a story to tell about Ned. Go get dressed and come down and say hello. You can have something to eat. I've made some sandwiches.'

I shrugged him off.

'If they haven't found his body, how do they know he's dead? I'm going back to my bedroom. I hate the lot of them. I want them all to go home.'

The following days drifted into a hopeless routine. I would go down to an empty kitchen; the television would be blaring out in the living room. I would make Mammy some breakfast then sit in silence as I ate mine. After that, I would clean the house, make some bread then disappear out onto the beach before Daddy got up and the steady trickle of visitors arrived.

The mornings drifted by easily – at least I had something to do – but afternoons were a different matter; I mostly spent them on the beach, searching for Bridie and Seamus, and staring out to sea. Usually, I would sit on a large boulder with a U-shaped dip. Uncle Ned had called it the séanchai chair after the famous Irish storytellers of years gone by. Sitting there, he'd told me tales of kelpies and mermaids, selkies and naiads, and all about the underwater world of the sea fairies.

I believed every word.

As the weeks went by, the weather became colder. Uncle Ned had said that Jimmy had to fish further out in the colder weather as the fish swam deeper. Maybe Bridie and Seamus were fishing out there, too. I desperately needed to find them to ask them what happened to Uncle Ned and to say thank you for rescuing me, but they seemed to have disappeared off the face of the earth.

Today, as I walked down the shingle path, a sea fret hid my view of the sea, so I walked up and down the beach making small footprints in the sand.

Out of the mists, a figure appeared and for a split second my heart soared. I ran towards it until I got close enough to see it was only Jimmy Connolly.

'Hawarye, Noola?' he asked.

I could barely speak and choked back the tears.

'I'm terrible sad, Jimmy. Me stomach feels like it's full of knots and me head hurts all the time. I wish he'd taken me with him.'

'Sure, don't talk like that, child. Ye've all yer life ahead of ye. I remember when me old da went. Sure, I was crying all the time. Me mammy said, she said, "Jimmy, don't be sad for what you've lost; be happy for what you had." So then, when I'd feel sad, I'd remember all the fishing trips we went on, or the times he used to take me to the arcades in Ballybay. Sure, it always made me smile remembering and all that.'

I tried to smile.

'Thanks, Jimmy, but he's swimming to America, ye know.'

Jimmy gave a nervous laugh.

'He couldn't swim to America. It's thousands of miles away.'

I felt a physical pain, as if I'd been stabbed, and grabbed Jimmy's arm as my legs buckled.

Jimmy supported my weight to stop me from falling.

'He could've been taken by the siseesh, though. There was a mighty strong wind that day,' he said.

I could feel my breath quicken. 'D'ya think so Jimmy? Do you really think he could have been?' Jimmy looked down at the sand and put his hand on my shoulder.

'Would ye like some fish te take home with ye?'

'No, it's okay Jimmy. I don't eat fish anymore, and Mammy's started getting those microwave dinners delivered with the shopping. She says it's easier for me that way.'

A rare look of anger flashed across his face.

'I'll see ye later,' he said, walking away. He had his hands in his pockets, his shoulders were hunched and he kicked the sand all the way to his boat.

As I watched him go, Uncle Ned's words came back to me.

'I've heard of loads of people being taken by the siseesh; it's dangerous and not to be messed with.

The siseesh… of course, it was so obvious I couldn't believe I hadn't thought of it before. The night before he'd disappeared, Uncle Ned had dreamt he'd been carried off by the wind. Dingbat said the siseesh took people to the Otherworld. I had to find out where it was. I raced after Jimmy, catching him up as he was folding his fishing net into his boat.

'Jimmy, where's the Otherworld?' Jimmy carried on folding his nets and frowned.

'Why d'ya want to know?'

'Because if the siseesh took Uncle Ned, that's where he'll be.'

'I didn't say he was definitely taken by the siseesh, Noola. I said he could've been.'

'Well, if he has been, it'll have taken him to the Otherworld, so I need to find out where it is.'

Jimmy put the nets down and stared out to sea.

'The seanchai talk of another world, but I've yet to meet a man in Ireland who's ever been there.'

'Uncle Ned believed in it,' I said, 'and I believe in it too.'

He picked his net up again, avoiding my eyes.

'Jimmy, what's a meremortal?'

'That's a strange question Noola. Why d'ya ask?' he said, looking puzzled.

'Because Uncle Ned has seen the fairies, and he said that fairies weren't for the eyes of meremortals.'

Jimmy sighed.

'He meant that they're not for the eyes of humans.'

I jumped up and down, clapping my hands.

'So that proves it.'

'Proves what?' said Jimmy.

'That he has the magic in him, so he must be connected to the Otherworld and he could've been taken by the siseesh.'

Jimmy dropped his head and looked away.

'Go home now Noola. I have to gather these nets before the rain comes.'

I ran across the beach to the cliffs to look for Bridie and Seamus. Maybe they'd know how to get to the Otherworld.

At the bottom of the cliffs, I found Bridie's friend, Winnie, sitting on a boulder, finishing off the remains of a large herring.

'Winnie,' I asked, 'have ye seen Bridie and Seamus today?'

'You've just missed them,' she answered. 'Not half an hour ago they headed off south for the winter. There's a strong south westerly due. I'm off miself now I've finished this bit o' dinner. You take care now and I'll see you in the springtime.'

Winnie took off, flying away from the cliffs and out to sea.

I dropped to my knees and watched her until she became a pinprick on the horizon. A solitary tear rolled down my cheek dripping off my chin.

Uncle Ned's stock of whiskey gradually dwindled until three weeks after he disappeared, his shed was empty.

His friends stopped coming and the house became unbearably quiet apart from the noise from the television, and the arguments which were getting worse by the day.

Daddy had started staying out, only coming home at bedtime, when the arguments would start all over again.

Apart from the arguments, nothing much else happened.

Until the day the men came to take the television.

There were three of them. Two of them were wearing T-shirts. They had bald heads and tattoos all over their arms; the third man was wearing a suit.

I stood behind Daddy who stood in the kitchen doorway, his arms folded, glowering at the men. Mammy was sat on the sofa, biting her nails.

'Here Paddy, help me with this,' said one of the tattooed men, picking up one side of the sofa, forcing Mammy to roll onto the floor. She sat very still with her arms folded, until they picked up the television.

I bit my lip to stop myself from smiling as Mammy screamed at the men.

'Leave that where it is.'

Running into the kitchen, she came back with a rolling pin.

'I'm warning you, put it down,' she screamed, running across the room and jumping onto Paddy's back. Clinging round his neck, she started to hit him over the head with it.

'Ah, get off me, ye great fat lump,' said Paddy, casually flicking her away as if she were an annoying fly. She landed on the floor with a thump, buried her head in her hands and sobbed.

As I watched, I felt detached, as if I was watching a scene from a soap opera.

I was glad they took the television.

I stayed in my bedroom for the rest of the day. Eventually, holding the faded photo of Uncle Ned in my hand, I fell into an uneasy sleep. I dreamt of Uncle Ned. He was swimming through the sea and he looked so tired. His face was blue from the cold and he seemed to be struggling. He held out a hand and I grabbed it. 'I'm here, Uncle Ned!' I screamed, pulling his hand, trying to save him from the crashing waves, but he was impossibly heavy.

I woke up sweating and trembling, the bright moonlight flooding my room. I looked out at the still, inky blackness of the sea, broken only by the glittering path of silver light leading up to the lonely moon hanging in the sky. A solitary star shone next to it.

'Where are you Uncle Ned?' I whispered into the darkness, as a sea-scented breeze wafted in through my open window.

I pulled out my journal and by the light of the moon, added something to my bucket list: FIND UNCLE NED.

I lay on my bed and thought about the dream. I'd never seen Uncle Ned swim, not once. I'd only ever seen him paddle, and besides, he'd never have left me of his own free will. Jimmy was right.

I'd been stupid to think he could swim all that way.

It was many hours before I drifted off to sleep again.

The following morning, I was woken by raised voices in the hallway. I peeped round the banister to see Mammy and Daddy. Mammy had her coat on and a suitcase beside her.

'You'll have to take her with you. I have to work and there'll be no one to mind her,' said Daddy.

'London's no place for a child, and I'll have to work, too, now you've gambled away everything,' Mammy replied, jabbing her finger into his chest.

'Well, take her to her grandma and grandad then. Let them look after her,' said Daddy.

'Her grandad's not there anymore; he left years ago,' said Mammy.

My heart started to beat wildly and my cheeks burned. I was being dumped, marooned, abandoned! I started to cry, louder and louder until at last they realised I was there.

'For goodness' sake, Noola, stop wailing like a banshee. Go and pack some things. The taxi will be here in a few minutes,' said Mammy. I dressed quickly, grabbed an old handbag, shoved in some underwear and socks, along with my notebook and the faded photo of Uncle Ned, and ran downstairs. I called out,

'Daddy, Daddy… where are ye?' Daddy was nowhere to be seen. I ran outside and jumped into the taxi just in time as it sped off down the lane and out into the open countryside.

Chapter
8

The Journey

As I watched out of the taxi window, I saw the craggy, boulder-strewn landscape of the west coast of Ireland soften into miles and miles of green. An endless carpet of grass, sprinkled with little white thatched cottages.

As if travelling through time, the cottages became bungalows. It was a beautiful October day and the sun glimmered through the trees, casting shadows of monsters on the fields. I'd never been further than Ballybay and I'd never been in a car. Speeding along the winding roads was beginning to make me feel sick. The initial rush of excitement had gone and I wished I was back home.

A feeling of panic crept over me. I was leaving Ballybay behind along with Uncle Ned. As the car slowed down in the busy traffic, I stared out of the window.

'Mammy, I need to go home. I should be on the beach in case Uncle Ned comes back,' I said. She stared at me with her mouth hanging open and shook her head rolling her eyes, she turned to look out of the window as the car came to a standstill outside the railway station. I got out just in time and threw up all over the pavement.

'Good God child, get in there before somebody sees it,' she said, paying the taxi driver and shoving me into the station.

The train to Dublin and the airport was just about to leave as we got on and found an empty seat.

'Where are we going, Mammy?' I asked.

'I'm going to London and you're going to stay with your grandma in Pebble Bridge.'

'Where's Pebble Bridge?' I asked, 'Is it near London?'

'No, it's in the North of England, in Yorkshire.' She looked out of the window and carried on as if she was talking to herself.

'It's a strange place, a very strange place. You'll fit in there. I never did.' She turned round to look at me.

'Now be quiet while I read my magazine.'

I gazed around at the other people on the train and realised they were staring at me. 'Mammy, why are those people staring at me?' I asked. Mammy turned round and glared at the other passengers.

'Did you bring your hat?' I put my hand in the pocket of my grey, wool coat and pulled out my colourful stripy bobble hat, waving it in front of her.

'Put it on and hide your ears. When you get older you need to get something done about those ears. They can do amazing things with plastic surgery these days.'

I pulled the hat on. I felt sick and the pain in my stomach that I'd had since Uncle Ned disappeared felt worse. My thoughts drifted back to that terrible day. It seemed so long ago and far away now, but maybe if I could find out where the Otherworld was, I'd be able to find him. My medallion glowed, warming me, and it felt like a sign.

Maybe it was leading me towards him. I watched as the rain lashed the window, the raindrops hitting the glass and racing each other to nowhere. Eventually, the chugging noise of the train made me drowsy and I drifted off to sleep.

When I woke, the train was pulling into the station in Dublin. It was raining harder than ever now as we ran to the bus station

to catch the bus to the airport. The crowds of people and towering buildings seemed a million miles from Ballybay.

'I don't like it here,' I said. 'I feel like I've landed on another planet.'

'Look, we'll be on the plane soon and we'll get something to eat. You'll feel better then,' said Mammy.

The airport was crowded. I leaned against a large pillar while Mammy went to buy the tickets. I shut my eyes and heard someone playing a tune on a penny whistle. Peering round the other side of the pillar, I saw a tiny man dressed in a bright green suit. The man looked at me and smiled. He had a round, cheerful face with two rosy red cheeks and a dimple in his chin. He tipped his hat.

'Top o'the morning to ye,' he said.

I wasn't surprised. By now, I was used to unusual confrontations. I smiled back.

'Hawarye? I'm Noola O'Brien. Who are you?'

'Hamish O'blivion. Original Irish leprechaun. Nice to meet you.'

'It's nice to meet you, too. I've never met a leprechaun before. There aren't any where I live…, not many people, either, come to think of it. Just rocks and boulders. Shouldn't you be in a wood or a field, if you're a leprechaun?'

'I do live in a wood, but I come here busking every day. Very lucrative, it is. The Yanks love me. But what brings you here? It's not the usual mode of transport for your lot, I must say. Don't your lot usually travel by siseesh?'

'What do you mean? I'm with my mammy. She's gone to get the tickets for the aeroplane. We're going to England.'

'But you're pixies. Pixies don't travel on aeroplanes.'

'No, we're not pixies.'

'Yes, you are. I spotted you both as soon as you came in. We don't get many pixies in here.'

I frowned. Why did everyone keep calling me a pixie.

'Your mammy's had surgery, too, by the look of her ears. They're very red.' I turned round to see Mammy rushing towards me.

'It's not just her ears that are red, she looks rather cross,' said the leprechaun. Mammy grabbed me by the arm and pulled me away.

'What on earth do you think you're doing? Don't talk to anything - I mean, anyone. I mean, just don't talk at all.'

She glanced back at the leprechaun, a look of terror on her face.

'Come on,' she said, pulling me all the way to the waiting area for the plane.

The plane journey was as bad as the taxi. The weather was stormy and turbulence caused the plane to bounce up and down.

After what seemed like a week, the plane landed and we caught a taxi to the station. We didn't have to wait long for the train to Pebble Bridge.

The seats were arranged in such a way that we were sat opposite a mysterious woman dressed in a colourful tie-dyed maxi dress with matching flowers in her hair. Her face was pitch black, which only accentuated the whites of her huge eyes. They shone from its darkness, twinkling with mischief.

Mammy had fallen asleep, but I was daydreaming trying to imagine what Grandma's house would look like.

The woman smiled at me. She opened a packet of chocolate éclairs and nudged the bag in front of me.

'Want a sweet?' she said. I hadn't eaten much all day and I was starving. Despite being told by Uncle Ned that I shouldn't take sweets from strangers, I took one.

It tasted wonderful.

'What's your name, child?' the woman asked.

'Fionnuala Isabel Maddison Rose O'Brien,' I answered.

'Wow, that's a big name for such a little girl!'

'Yes, that's what my Uncle Ned used to say.'

'Where you going child?' the woman asked, pushing the bag of sweets towards me. I took another sweet.

'I'm going to stay with my grandma in Pebble Bridge.'

The woman threw back her head and laughed, showing the inside of her mouth, which was bright pink in stark contrast to her black face. Her back teeth were gold and her front teeth were studded with diamonds.

'You are Izzy and Pixie's granddaughter! I thought your mamma looked familiar. Yes, I knew it. You have the magic in you, for sure, and you're the image of your grandad.'

'How do you know my grandma and grandad?' I asked, unable to hide my amazement.

'After I came from Africa, many years ago, I went to the witch's college with your grandma. Me, Lula and Izzy. My we had some fun.'

'Witch's college? You're a w-w-witch?' I swallowed the toffee which had wedged in my throat. 'Does that mean my grandma's a witch, too?' I croaked.

'One of the best. Mi name's Juli - Juli Anabaluloo. Your grandma was a wiz with the potions. Me, transfiguration was my bag.' The woman shut her eyes and began to hum. She started to rock from side to side, swaying and trembling.

After a few moments, her hand cupped over a drowsy wasp walking along the table in front of us. The humming became chanting and her eyes rolled in their sockets. She rubbed the wooden necklace round her neck with her other hand.

'Mumbago Tibiago Malawi Dijango,' chanted the woman. She lifted her hand and there, in place of the wasp, was a huge hairy spider the size of a tarantula.

I was unable to speak. As I stared at the spider, Juli picked it up by its leg and threw it into the aisle, where it ran under the seat opposite.

'Wow, that was amazing,' I said, staring open-mouthed. She emptied the last of the sweets onto the table, gesturing to me to take one.

'Thanks,' I said, trying to take in what had just happened.

'Learned how to do that in Africa,' she said in a matter-of-fact kind of voice.

'Why did you leave Africa?' I asked. 'They must have some wonderful schools if they can teach you how to do things like that.'

'Had to leave in a hurry. I was having a spot of bother with the locals. So, I caught the siseesh. But that was a long time ago now.'

I leaned forward, my heart thundering. If Juli had been on the siseesh, she might know how to get to the Otherworld.

'My Uncle Ned was taken by the siseesh on my birthday. Where would he be now?'

Juli shrugged.

'Could be anywhere - it travels round. Let me woogle it,' she said, taking a furry orange hold-all from under her seat. She put on some round, red glasses and took something out of her bag. It looked like a book, covered in beautiful iridescent scales. The scales twinkled and glowed, projecting luminous colours onto the train windows and lighting up the sky beyond. It seemed to come from another world.

Seeing the look of amazement on my face, she smiled. 'You like it?'

'It's lovely. What is it?

'It's a compoculum, a sort of cross between a computer and a crystal ball. The case is made from dragon scales.'

'Wow, where do the dragon scales come from?' I asked.

'Far away and long ago,' she said, staring into space.

I wondered if she was having me on.

As she opened the compoculum, a mist appeared to rise from it. Her massive eyes grew even bigger.

"Otherworld, events and festivals,' she said, tapping the keyboard. She smiled at me, her expression gleeful. 'You're in luck, child. It will be in Pebble Bridge next year, March 20th Ostara Fair.' Juli looked at the screen as if she was gazing into a crystal ball. Her eyes clouded over and I noticed a troubled expression flicker across her face. She closed it as the train braked.

'Next stop Pendle,' said a disembodied voice over the tannoy. She took the necklace from round her neck and gave it to me.

'Take this, child. I think you're going to need it. Guard it well. It's very powerful.' I took the necklace and stuffed it into my coat pocket.

Juli got up and picked up her bag.

'Yours is the next stop, child. Don't miss it. Goodbye and good luck,' she said.

I didn't want her to go; I had too many questions that needed answering.

'Juli, is my grandad a pixie?' I asked, fearful of the answer.

Juli laughed a deep throaty laugh.

'Of course he is,' she said, disappearing through the sliding doors.

I felt my ears. I was the granddaughter of a real life witch and a pixie. How awesome! I'd always known I wasn't like other kids, now everything was starting to make sense. Uncle Ned used to call me his little pixie princess - he must have known.

I looked at Mammy, who snored softly with her mouth open. I stood up and looked at the scar tissue on the tops of her ears and swallowed hard. I counted the months until March. Six whole months until I could find Uncle Ned. I couldn't wait six months.

At the next station, the train stopped again. The noise of the train braking woke Mammy. I looked outside to see a long sign illuminated in the darkness,

WELCOME TO PEBBLE BRIDGE.

Outside the station was a small car park flanked by tall trees. They were swaying in the wind, waving their branches as if welcoming the visitors. Mammy stared up at them, wide-eyed and terrified. She stood in the middle of the road, frantically waving her hands like a mad woman and flagged down a taxi. She pushed me inside.

'How much?' she asked, thrusting the address in front of the driver. I watched her pay him and waited for her to get in.

She didn't. She just stuck her head inside and said,

'Goodbye, Noola. Be good for your grandma. Tell her I'll come and see you sometime.' Mammy slammed the taxi door and rushed into the station without looking back.

Chapter

9

'Grandma, are you really a witch?'

The rain lashed down and the wind howled as I stood on the doorstep of Grandma's cottage.

'Please let her be in; please let it be the right house,' I whispered.

I couldn't reach the door knocker so I looked round in the darkness and spotted an old bucket. I dragged it over to the door and turned it upside down to stand on. Stretching up, I knocked as loudly as I could.

As I stood shivering on the bucket, I heard a noise behind me. It seemed to be coming from the other side of the fence.

I turned round to see what looked like a man peering over. I could just about make out shoulders and a head.

Staring at me out of the darkness were two bright red glowing eyes.

I started to shake. I stood, rigid with fear, not taking my eyes off the shadowy figure until, after a few moments, I heard a noise from behind the door, then a muffled voice. 'Who's there?'

'Fionnuala Isabel Maddison Rose O'Brien,' I shouted, trying to make myself heard over the howling wind. Getting down from the bucket, I stood trembling on the doorstep. I was just about to meet a real live witch who might turn me into a slug or something worse.

The door opened and I met my grandma for the first time. I gave a little involuntary jump. I'd seen this woman before. This was the woman I had dreamt about, the woman in the purple and blue cloak in the woods. She didn't look like a witch. Her skin was as smooth as an apple, not wrinkled and wizened like you'd expect a witch's to be. Her small round glasses magnified her blue-grey eyes. Same as Mammy's – not mine.

'Are you Isabel Flynn?' I asked.

'Yes, I am. Who are you?'

'Fionnuala Isabel Maddison Rose O'Brien. I'm your granddaughter. Very pleased to meet you.' I held out my hand to shake Grandma's and curtseyed at the same time. I'd seen people do this on the TV and it seemed the right thing to do.

Grandma swayed with shock, she took off her glasses and wiped them. Putting them back on she peered out at me and her hand fluttered towards her chest.

'Who are you with? Who's brought you?' she asked me, poking her head out of the door to see who else was there. The shadowy figure had disappeared.

'No one, I'm on my own. Mammy's gone to London,' I said.

'Come in, child, before you catch your death of cold. Take off your coat and go into the room.'

I took off my coat, passed it to Grandma and went into the front room. I gazed around in amazement. What I had expected to see was a black cat and a cauldron bubbling on a stove; what I actually saw looked as if it wouldn't be out of place in a gypsy caravan. Colourful throws and cushions covered the sofas and a huge cage with a beautiful red and blue parrot inside filled one corner. It felt cosy and warm, not like our living room in Ballybay.

'Hello, pleased to meet you. I didn't know we were expecting visitors,' said a voice from the other side of the room. I jumped back in surprise. Hanging on the wall was

a living tree with two branch-like arms and a twiggy hand
holding the TV remote.

'H-Hawarye?' I'm Noola. I've c-come from Ireland,' I
stuttered, edging my way around the sofa with my back to
the wall. I sat back in one of the large armchairs, not taking
my eyes off the strange sight of a talking tree hanging on a
living room wall. As I scanned the room, Uncle Ned's words
came back to me and I understood.

'Your family's very unusual, to say the least.'

In front of the armchair, a big black wood-burning stove
glowed brightly. I watched the flames flicker and dance,
casting shadows on the walls, and my eyelids drooped. I
shook myself, too afraid to shut my eyes as I watched the
tree flicking through the TV channels. The heat of the stove,
however, made me drowsy; I felt more exhausted than I'd
ever been in my life.

The next thing I remember is waking up with daylight streaming through the window to the steady rhythmic snoring of the tree. I was on the chair, covered in a colourful patchwork quilt, with the fire still burning and the parrot watching me warily. I went into the small kitchen but Grandma was nowhere to be seen. I opened a doorway off the kitchen and went down some wooden steps into a brightly lit cellar. Grandma was dressed in a white coat and was pouring some liquid into a bottle.

'Oh, you're awake. I'll make you some breakfast in a little while. I've just got to finish this for a customer. He'll be collecting it this evening,' she said.

The room looked like a laboratory. On one side, the walls were shelved and on them were hundreds of little empty bottles; on the other side of the room were crates full of the same bottles, filled and waiting for collection. All the bottles were numbered and beautifully decorated. I was attracted to some full of red liquid with little hearts on the label. The hearts pulsed and the liquid glittered and moved. I picked one up and looked closer.

'What's this one for, Grandma?' I asked.

Grandma looked at me from over her spectacles.

'That's a love philtre. It's an affecting potion; it alters the way people feel. It's made from sea serpent bones and dried hogthistle. I mix it to a powder, then add blueberry juice to make it palatable, and finally a simpering twert. All you need then is a strand of hair from the person who's looking for love, mix it in, and give it to the person they want to fall in love with them. It works a treat. I've been invited to loads of weddings from the customers who've used it.'

'Wow! Do you have sea serpents in Pebble Bridge, Grandma?' I asked. She tutted.

'Don't be silly child. I get them off the Internet.'

'What's a simpering twert, Grandma?'

'My word, you do ask a lot of questions. Go upstairs and talk to Buddy. He's very interesting.'

She turned her back on me and carried on filling the bottle. I didn't want to leave the cellar. Every few seconds, a bright light shot out of one of the bottles like a firework, lighting up the ceiling with an eerie green, blue or purple glow. It reminded me of the time that me and Uncle Ned had seen the Northern Lights when we went on a visit to his cousin in Sligo. Grandma looked up.

'Go on then,' she said. I went upstairs to the living room where Buddy, the tree spirit, was watching the local news. The newsreader talked about a shopping complex about to be built in Pebble Bridge. Buddy flailed his twiggy arms about and shouted.

'Don't they realise what they're doing to the planet? They can't carry on with industrial and economic growth indefinitely. Don't they realise the impact all these new buildings are having on the world's resources? It's insane. One day, the world's going to explode – BOOM! – into millions of tiny pieces and don't expect us trees to rescue then you stupid people.'

The parrot, who up until now had been asleep with his head under his wing, woke with a fright.

'What's happening? What's happening?' he said, flapping his wings in alarm at Buddy's words.

'Is the world ending? Get me out, get me out!' Grandma came into the room to see what all the commotion was about.

'Oh really, Buddy, stop frightening Jonjo with your silly talk. He's nervous enough as it is without you making him worse.'

'Why is Jonjo so nervous?' I asked.

'His tree was chopped down while he was still in it. He was very young and he's never recovered from the trauma.'

'I thought parrots lived in hot countries. Are there many parrots in Pebble Bridge?' I asked.

'Jonjo came here many years ago with his mate, Juno. They came from the tropical rain forests of Brazil. When they got here, they couldn't stand the cold. They used to sit on my windowsill looking at the fire, so I took them in.'

'Where's his mate now?'

'She was a very clever parrot but she was stolen from me a long time ago now. it made Jonjo very sad.'

'Poor Jonjo, no wonder he's so nervous.

Who would do such a terrible thing?' Grandma's eyes became glassy and she sighed heavily.

'Your grandad took her when he left.' I could see from the look on Grandma's face that this was a touchy subject.

'But if you're a witch, couldn't you turn him into a slug or something and steal her back?'

'Believe me, I've thought about it but I'm not much good at transfiguration and besides, he has a young family now and it wouldn't be fair on them.'

Grandma turned and went into the kitchen banging a pan onto the stove. I got the message. The subject was closed.

We had breakfast at a little table in the kitchen. I looked round the small room with its low beamed ceiling.

Dozens of jars, filled with scented herbs and exotic spices, were crammed onto stout wooden shelves. Two small windows looked onto an overgrown garden flanked by a tall green fence at the bottom.

Grandma placed a large plate of bacon and eggs in front of me and I felt like I hadn't eaten for a week. The food looked delicious but Uncle Ned always told me not to start until everyone else was eating - it's bad manners - so I waited for Grandma to sit down.

'How is your Mammy anyway?' she said, sitting down with her breakfast.

'Fine, thank you,' I said, starting to make a sandwich with my bacon and eggs.

'She's gone to London because she needs to find a job.'

Grandma tutted and I could tell she was annoyed. Maybe in England people don't make sandwiches out of their breakfasts. I took a bite. The bacon was delicious – crispy, just the way Uncle Ned made it. I noticed Grandma wasn't eating, just moving the food around her plate with her fork.

'Who's the man in the photo that's in your bag?' she said.

I swallowed down the half eaten mouthful of food.

'That's my Uncle Ned. He looked after me while Mammy watched the television. He went away on my birthday, then Daddy came home and he'd spent all the money on the horses so the men took the television and Mammy went to London and I came here to stay with you.'

Grandma's face sagged, just the way Mammy's does. I could see the resemblance between them and it struck me that I didn't look a bit like either of them.

'Are you really a witch, Grandma?' I asked.

'Yes, I am. I'm what you call a hedge witch.'

'I met another witch on the train. She was called Juli Anabaluloo. She said you were at college together.'

Grandma looked shocked. She stared out of the window, a faraway look in her eyes.

'It's funny how Juli only appears when there's a crisis in my life. The last time I saw her was when your mammy ran off. It's as if she knows.'

'She turned a wasp into a huge hairy spider right in front of me,' I said, shivering at the thought of it.

'Juli was top of the class, a brilliant student, a very talented witch. Her talismans were very powerful. She used to get us into all sorts of trouble. She got kicked out in the end for turning the teacher into a rat. She turned her back again five minutes later, but not before the rat had created havoc running all over the school.'

'I've never been to school,' I said.

Grandma dropped her fork and stared at me.

'Never been to school? But that's ridiculous. How old are you?'

'I've just turned eleven, but I can read and write. Uncle Ned taught me. We didn't have broadband, though, so I don't know how to work computers.' Grandma looked at me in dismay as I carried on.

'Juli said she came to England on the siseesh.'

Grandma got up, scraped her food into the bin and put her plate in the sink. She hadn't eaten a thing.

'Siseesh, my bunions! She came on a plane, same as you,' she said, slamming her plate onto the draining board.

'Don't believe everything people tell you. Now finish your breakfast. We need to go into town to get you some things. I've rung the social workers and they said you need to go to school.' She carried on with the dishes muttering to herself,

'Not sending the child to school. How could she be so irresponsible.'

I finished my breakfast in silence. Why was Grandma so mad? And why had she rung the social workers? I'd heard about them from the television. They put the children that nobody wanted in homes.

I didn't want to go in a home for unwanted children. And I didn't believe Grandma when she said that Juli hadn't come on the siseesh. It's as if she didn't believe it existed. But it does, I'd seen it, and Dingbat and Wombat had been on it.

My stomach was churning; even the prospect of going to school couldn't cheer me up. I had to find Uncle Ned.

Chapter
10

Lula Moon

I watched uneasily as Grandma stood in front of a mirror in the hallway putting on a strange-looking mask. The mask was made from some sort of rubber soft and pliable and very realistic, complete with wrinkles and moles. Grandma looked ten years older.

I wanted to ask if all witches wore masks to go shopping but sensed Grandma's bad mood and kept quiet.

As we walked into town, I looked up at the steep hills stretching up from the road on either side. The higgeldy-piggledy piggyback houses nestled into the hillside reminded me of barnacles clinging to a rock.

The smell of freshly baked bread wafted from a brightly painted shop, and all around me shop awnings clattered open, along the narrow twisty streets.

The air was muggy, one of those days when it threatens to rain but never does. I wished I hadn't worn my coat.

'I need a drink,' said Grandma.

'This mask is stifling me and sweat is trickling down my back. Come on, we'll go and see my friend Lula.'

We walked to a little square in the middle of town and down a side street where Grandma's friend owned a shop and café. The shop looked bright and inviting with its name "Mystic Moon" above the door.

On the sign was a picture of a cat sitting under the dark silhouette of a tree looking up at a full moon. Underneath the sign were the words: **LULA MOON, MYSTIC AND PSYCHIC, TAROT AND CRYSTALS.**

Inside, there was a strange overpowering smell. I read the sign. **INCENSE AND ESSENTIAL OILS** it said. There were little wicker baskets of crystals lined up, wind chimes hanging from every bit of ceiling, and paintings of witches and mythical creatures covered the walls; every conceivable space was full of interesting gifts and trinkets.

I gazed around. I had entered a fantasyland where anything was possible. A multi-coloured butterfly landed on my shoulder and I made a wish because I was in a magic place where wishes might come true.

I watched Lula bustling around the shop like a baby hippopotamus. She wore a brightly coloured kaftan covered in pictures of parrots and exotic plants. Her jet black hair looked like it had been dyed. It was tied high on her head in a bun with a fountain of dreadlocks interspersed with multi-coloured beads exploding from it like fireworks.

She started arranging a display of candles on the counter and looked at me, her head cocked to one side, as if she was trying to figure something out. In front of the display, a sign said, **MAGIC BUTTERFLY CANDLES.** One of the candles was lit and as it burned down, more brightly coloured butterflies were released from the wax. There were already three or four fluttering around the shop.

'They're beautiful,' I said.

Lula, sensing a sale, shoved one of the candles under Grandma's nose.

'I make them myself. They're scented, too. This one's bluebell and comfrey.'

A singeing smell filled the air, and the mask started to disintegrate. Grandma's eyelids started to droop and her nose melted into her mouth. Within seconds, she looked horrific. Lula screamed and hid under the counter. I watched in alarm as Grandma unhooked the melting mask and jumped up and down on it before it burst into flames. She leaned over the counter and looked at Lula.

'Lula, it's me, Isabel. What on earth do you think you were doing, putting that candle so close to my face?'

Lula appeared from under the counter, still shaking.

'What on earth were you doing, coming in here with that hideous mask on? You scared the living daylights out of me!'

'I had to be incognito. I've got a visitor, and I don't want every Tom, Dick and Harry knowing about it,' said Grandma, pushing me towards her.

'Hawarye? I'm Noola, pleased to meet you,' I said.

Lula looked at me and her mouth fell open.

'Well, there's no need to tell me who this is,' she said, grabbing me and pinning me so tightly to her huge chest, I thought I might suffocate.

'She's called Fionnuala. She's Bridget's daughter,' said Grandma.

'She turned up on my doorstep last night.' Lula pulled away and sat down so she was level with my face.

'Wow, she's the spitting image of…'

'My grandad,' I said, catching my breath. 'Juli Anabaluloo told me.'

'Where's Bridget?' asked Lula.

'Noola, go and have a look around the shop at all the lovely things,' said Grandma, pushing me towards a display of birds carved out of wood.

I was happy to look around. I wanted to buy everything I saw, but I made sure I could still hear what they were saying.

'Where is she then?' whispered Lula.

'She's not here, obviously. She didn't even call in to say hello, just dumped the child in a taxi and beggared off. Scared I wouldn't take her and then she'd have been stuck with her. What if I'd moved or something? It doesn't bear thinking about. And she hasn't got a stitch of clothing with her apart from what she's wearing.'

'Doesn't sound like Bridget's changed much; she was always the selfish one,' replied Lula.

'But that's not the worst of it,' said Grandma, taking a tissue out of her pocket and wiping her face. 'The child's never even been to school.'

Lula gasped.

'That's terrible. What are you going to do with her?'

I hid behind a pillar and peeped round.

'She can stay until the social workers can find her a home. I can't look after her. I wasn't much good as a parent first time around and I'm too old to do it all over again. And look at her, do I want a constant reminder of "him" every day.'

'I must admit she is the spitting image of Pixie, but she seems polite enough,' replied Lula.

'Yes, someone's taught her good manners. But she'd only end up leaving me like the rest of them. No, my days of getting attached to people are well and truly over. She'll have to go.'

My insides became heavy. Somehow the shop seemed to have lost its magic.

So, my hunch was right, Grandma didn't want me. Unexpected tears filled my eyes and ran down my cheeks. I wiped them away with my fists and walked over to the carved wooden birds. I thought of Uncle Ned and wished with all my heart that I was with him.

As I approached the birds, I could feel my heartbeat quicken. One of the birds was a seagull and it reminded me of home. I approached it warily. It stared straight at me and reflected in its glass eyes, I could see Ballybay, the cliffs and two seagulls circling in the warm Gulf Stream current flying towards the rocks.

Light slanting through a roof window cast a shadow of the birds onto the floor. The shadows flapped their wings like bird-shaped ghosts. Spooked, I went back to Grandma and Lula.

'Where do those birds come from, Lula?' I asked.

Lula bent down so she was at eye level with me.

'They're carved by your Grandma's assistant, Dillon Cobnutt. He's a wood elf, slightly mad, but very creative.'

'We'll go see him later,' said Grandma. 'Apart from being artistic, he's also a wizard on the computer. He orders my ingredients from all over the world. I'll get him to teach you how to use it.'

'You'll need to know for school,' said Lula.

'And I'll ask him if he'll give you one of his mobile phones; he's got dozens of them said Grandma. He gets a new model every few months.'

'All the kids have them nowadays,' said Lula.'

Grandma slumped into one of the café chairs.

'Make us a cup of tea, will you, Lula? I'm exhausted. I didn't sleep a wink last night.'

'Yes, and you can have one of my speciality hot chocolates with marshmallows, Fionnuala,' said Lula, wobbling away.

She came back a few minutes later with a tray. On it was a teapot and cups and a cup of hot chocolate topped with fresh cream and marshmallows, together with a large plate filled with cakes.

'Thanks, Lula. You can call me Noola, if you like,' I said, helping myself to a piece of chocolate cake. I was about to take a bite when I noticed a long black hair sticking out of it. I pulled the hair out, stuck it into the serviette Lula had given me, and stuffed it into my pocket. I didn't want to seem ungrateful, complaining and all that. Lula didn't notice. She was too busy scanning her mobile phone which she thrust into Grandma's face.

'Here, look at who came up on my dating site today. It's that dishy Doctor Dunderfield. I'm going to see if he wants to meet up.' Grandma rolled her eyes and tutted.

'Oh, honestly, Lula, he's awful. He's a right mummy's boy and incredibly vain. He'd never be interested in you.'

Lula scowled as Grandma carried on.

'If you want to go and see him, you can take Noola. The social worker said she has to have a booster injection and I can't be seen at the doctors. What would that do for my credibility? I'll mind the shop for you.'

'Oh, thank you. What a brilliant idea. Yes, of course I'll take her, it'll be my pleasure. Just let me know the date,' said Lula, squeezing my hand. The shop door pinged and Lula jumped up.

'Got to go, Isabel. Customers, bills to pay and all that.'

Grandma nudged me.

'Come on, we'll go now,' she said, but I couldn't move; I couldn't tear my eyes away from something shivering in the draught of the door above my head.

'What's that, Lula?' I asked.

'It's a dreamcatcher. They're like fishing nets, trawling our subconscious minds while we sleep,' she whispered, like she was afraid someone might hear.

'Do they work on nightmares?' I whispered back.

Lula raised one eyebrow and looked at Grandma.

'Yes, I suppose they would.'

She unhooked the dreamcatcher and gave it to me.

'Here, take it. It's a welcome present from me.

I'll get a box for you.'

I put the dreamcatcher in the box.

'Thanks, Lula. I'll let you know if it works.'

Chapter

II

The Dreamcatcher

We walked along the Main Street which was bustling with tourists, and passed a soap shop where rainbow-coloured bubbles floated through a window. Grandma stopped at the shop next door to it.

'Come on, I'll get you a few things so at least you'll have a change of clothes. I can't believe your mother never sent you with any,' she said, her voice sharp and irritated.

Inside the shop, I looked around. The shelves were filled with vases and bric-a-brac, jigsaws and books and opposite them were rails full of clothes.

'It doesn't look like any of the clothes shops Mammy goes to in Ballybay.'

'It's a charity shop,' said Grandma, pushing me towards a rack of children's clothes.

'Go on, choose some things. We haven't got all day.'

I picked a red jumper, a pink blouse and some jeans. The woman on the till stared at me, open mouthed. I took my hat out of my pocket and pulled it tightly over my ears. I put the clothes on the counter as Grandma flashed the woman an annoyed look, slammed the money down on the counter and hurried me out of the shop.

Further down the street, we passed an oriental woman sat on a mat on the pavement making origami wishing birds.

People were buying the birds and throwing them up into the sky, where they fluttered away with the rainbow bubbles.

Grandma grabbed my arm and yanked me into a shop doorway.

'One of my customers is across the road. Stand there and don't move,' she said. We waited near two tourists who were chatting. One of them looked at me and whispered,

'There are some strange-looking people in this town, Valerie. Some of them look like they've stepped straight out of a fairy tale.'

The customer Grandma had been trying to avoid had spotted her anyway and started to cross the road. She was a huge bow-legged woman. The man with her was short and skinny and about half her size. The woman looked like an overstuffed turkey. Rolls of skin hung from her chin and she wobbled when she walked. Huge globules of spit flew from her mouth as she spoke.

'Is our special hair-removing remedy ready, Isabel?' she asked. I bobbed up and down, trying to avoid the barrage of frothy spit flying from the woman's mouth.

'I'll have it ready for Saturday, if you want to collect it,' said Grandma. The small skinny man interrupted.

'I'll pick it up Friday, if that's okay? Our Rodney will be in a right strop if he doesn't get it before the weekend.' And with that, the pair waddled off.

'Who are they, Grandma, and why do they need a special hair-removing remedy?' I asked.

'That's Liberty and Bob Gobbit. They're goblins. They need my special remedy to stop hair growing all over them. I put in my special ingredients and then a hair from each of their heads. They'd be as hairy as a bunch of badgers within a week if they didn't get it. They've a son called Rodney. He's a right bully, a real bad egg.'

'But how come goblins live in Pebble Bridge? I thought they lived in the woods.'

'Pebble Bridge is an old mill town. When the mills shut down the workers all left, leaving the houses empty. Nobody wanted the houses so the goblins came out of the woods to live in them.'

'Don't the humans that live here mind?' I asked.

'No, not at all The quirkiness of the place attracts the tourists. It helps the economy.'

'Well, that woman was right. There are some strange-looking people in Pebble Bridge Grandma.'

'Yes,' she said, looking at me curiously, almost smiling.

'There certainly are.'

We walked to the edge of town, where the local school was set back from the main street.

It was playtime and Grandma chatted to the headmaster while I stood biting my nails and watching the children play. Some of the kids whispered and pointed and Uncle Ned's words came back to me: Kids don't like other kids who are different; they like to fit in.

Mammy said I would fit in here, but I wasn't so sure.

When we arrived home, Grandma walked straight past the gate of her cottage.

'Come on, I'll take you to meet Dillon. I need to order some more carvings for Lula and I haven't seen Sorrel for ages,' she said.

As we walked across the bridge to the other side of the canal and climbed the steps to the woods, the weak autumn sunlight glimmered through the battalions of trees that glowed for miles along both sides of the valley. From burnt orange to copper to deep muddy brown, they looked like a brilliant technicolour army.

We reached the clearing where a tiny man was chopping wood and something flew past my ears. There was a hiss, like air coming out of a balloon, then a crack as the thing that had flown past hit a tree.

'What on earth was that?' said Grandma.

The man looked up. 'It's Dillon. He's addicted to those berries from the bogglestrop bush. They give him horrendous wind and he's flying around like a B52 bomber, crashing into all the tree spirits. He'll be getting an ASBO from the wood warden if he's not careful. He's an adrenaline junkie. I think that's the modern word for it. We would have called him downright reckless years ago, a crazy lunatic,' he said wiping his brow.

'Well, I've got loads of remedies that need bottling and Lula needs some more wood carvings, so that should keep him out of mischief for a while.'

'Thanks, Isabel. I don't know what we'd do without you.'
He turned towards me and smiled.

'And who've you brought with you today? She looks familiar.'

'She's my granddaughter, Fionnuala O'Brien. Bridget's daughter.

Noola, this is Sorrel, Dill's father.'

I looked at him closely. He wasn't much bigger than me. His face was lined and crinkly like the bark of an old tree. He seemed very kind. I held out my hand.

'Pleased to meet you,' I said.

'You've got lovely manners for one so young, and I can see you're Pixie Flynn's granddaughter. You look just like him,' he said, taking my hand.

'She could be your apprentice, Isabel. You've been looking for one for ages.'

I stood very still, trying to contain my excitement. A witch's apprentice would surely be able to get to the Otherworld. Grandma ignored his suggestion. Her eyes had gone hard.

'Don't forget to tell Dill to bring some more carvings tomorrow; Lula's nearly sold out,' she said.

As they were speaking, Dill appeared, a strange, glazed look in his eyes. He staggered into the clearing and landed in a heap in front of us, letting go one last enormous blast of wind before setting off into a fit of drunken giggles.

'We'll be away home now. I'll see you in the morning, nice and early, Dill,' said Grandma, stepping over him and pulling me behind her. We stopped off at the bogglestrop bush where Grandma filled a bag with berries.

'You never know, these might come in useful for something,' she said.

We got home as the day darkened. The rain that had threatened to fall all day came down and thunder rolled around the valley.

'You can stay in your mammy's old room while you're here,' said Grandma, climbing the stairs in front of me.

The tiny room had a single bed and a wardrobe piled up to the ceiling with soft toys and games. The only window looked out onto the canal below and next door's garden and kitchen window. Dangling from the curtain pole was a wind chime made of glass with two dolphins jumping over a wave. In an instant, I returned to the Friday a few weeks before Uncle Ned disappeared and remembered him laughing and shouting at the dolphins in the bay. A heaviness crushed my chest like a dense sea fog, making it hard to breathe so I sat down on the bed.

Grandma opened the wardrobe, got out some sheets and a pillow and put them beside me.

'I'll change the bed later. I haven't been in here for such a long time,' she said, picking up a picture frame from the dressing table. In it, was a picture of Mammy as a little girl. I looked at it with her. Even when she was little, Mammy looked sad. Grandma's face clouded over and I reckoned she was remembering - same as me.

She sniffed.

'Can I hang up my dreamcatcher Grandma?' I asked.

'Yes, I suppose so, but don't be making yourself too comfortable,' she said. 'And don't be long, tea will be arriving soon. I'm ordering a pizza.'

That night, I had a nightmare. It was the same nightmare.

The one with Uncle Ned, only this time he wasn't in the sea - he was on the beach with sand swirling round him, the sea lapping over his feet.

'Get up, Uncle Ned. The tide's coming in,' I screamed.' I could hear the sea booming onto the sand, getting nearer with every wave, but I couldn't reach him. 'Get up, please,' I screamed.

I woke up with Grandma shaking me. 'For goodness' sake, what on earth's the matter? The neighbours will think I'm murdering you.'

'I'm sorry, Grandma, I didn't mean to wake you,' I said, pulling a blanket round me. The terror of the nightmare had left me soaked with sweat and shivering. Grandma turned off the light and shut the door.

'Go back to sleep, we've got a busy day tomorrow.'

I tried to steady my breathing, then lay awake for a long time until daylight started to creep through the curtains. Something moving caught my eye. The dreamcatcher was spinning.

I jumped up and pulled the tassels which hung from the circular cobweb of threads until it stopped. It was glowing like a miniature TV. The threads of the dreamcatcher were no longer there.

Uncle Ned was.

As he lay motionless on the sand, the clouds parted and a shaft of light lit up the scene, shining on Uncle Ned as if he was the main actor at the end of a performance. Moments later, the sand started to swirl, hiding my view. Then it stopped suddenly, leaving the beach deserted. Uncle Ned was gone.

As I watched, fascinated, the pain and grief returned. A physical pain as if someone had punched me in the stomach.

By the time I was greeted by the dawn chorus outside my window, I was certain: he had been taken by the siseesh. But I had no idea where it had taken him, or how I would find him.

Chapter

12

Dillon Cobnutt

A h, Dill, come and meet Noola. She's my
granddaughter, Bridget's girl,' said Grandma as
Dillon Cobnutt bounded through the door.

'Well, look at youuu! Ye look just like your grandad.
Poppa told me all about you.' Grandma frowned, but Dill
laughed.

'Well she does, Izzy. She's the
image of him.'

'I want you to teach her how
to use the computer so she
can order some clothes online.
I haven't got time to go trailing
round the shops.'

I couldn't take my eyes off Dill. By now
I was used to meeting strange people,
but he had to be the strangest of the
lot. Grandma had told me he was
thirty, but he looked much younger,
scrawny-looking and not much
taller than me. As he spoke, his huge
brown eyes flickered constantly, and his
face looked like the face of a puppet moulded
from papier-mâché. His pointed nose and ears,

and shaved head added to his doll-like appearance. He was hopping from one foot to the other, like a jerboa.

While Grandma was busy in the kitchen, Dill took me into an office with a large window, that looked out onto the front garden.

'How d'ya like Pebble Bridge?' he asked, twirling round three times on the office chair.

'It's lovely, small, and cute, and the people seem nice.'

'Some of them are, but some of them aren't,' he said, jumping up onto the ledge and opening the window. Putting his fingers to his mouth, he let out a long piercing whistle.

'Have you met Beezlebag yet?'

'Who's Beezlebag?' I asked.

'Lives next door. He's a creeper. Weaslebag, I call him, coz he's as nasty as a bag of weasels. He was snooping round in the woods today. I don't know what he was doing but you can bet he was up to no good.'

'That must be the man I saw the night I arrived. He's scary,' I said. As we were speaking, a large black raven appeared, landing on the window ledge. Dill poked a piece of paper through the window towards it.

'Take this note to Poppa. 'I'm staying over today, got lots to do and I'm having tea with Izzy.' He took a biscuit out of his

pocket and gave it to the bird, who flew off with it in its beak, gripping the note with its claws.

'That's Zach, my bird. I only have the feathered kind,' he said, winking at me and spinning round on the chair again.

'Right, come on then. Let's show you how it's done.'

He switched on the computer and became quiet.

I watched him. Concentrating on the computer had calmed him down and he was focused and still. After an hour showing me what to do, he let me have a go.

'Right, here's the search bar. Ask it a question - anything you like.'

'I asked the only question on my mind.

'How do I get to the Otherworld?' Dill looked puzzled.

'Why do you want to know that?'

I sniffed.

'Personal reasons,' I said.

'I can tell you the answer to that one. The Otherworld moves around. To find out where it's going to be next, you need a compoculum, but they're very rare and expensive. Difficult to get hold of unless you're very powerful and you've got loads of money.'

I sighed. Juli hadn't been having me on. I really would have to wait six months to find Uncle Ned.

Grandma shouted that dinner was ready, causing Dill to spin wildly on the chair again until it threw him off and he landed on the floor, laughing hysterically. He's mad, I thought. 'He's on his way to crazy town.

During dinner, Dill became calm again.

'I'll teach you how to do emails tomorrow, then you can email your folks,' he said.

'Oh, it's okay, I don't know where they are. Mammy's in London and Daddy's travelling with his job.'

'What about your uncle? Dill could teach you how to Zoom and you could tell him where you are, then he could come and collect you,' said Grandma.

'No, it's okay. Uncle Ned doesn't know how to work computers,' I said, my voice quivering.

'Well, come to ours for tea tomorrow. I'll show you my computer. It's the newest on the market,' said Dill.

'Oh, talking of computers, Dill, would you order me some more desiccated scuttlebugs? I've run out. I've been using loads for my new acne remedy. It's selling like hot cakes,' said Grandma.

'Yeah, sure. I'll order them tomorrow. I've found a new supplier They're heaps bigger and I can get them at a much better price,' he replied.

After Dill had gone home, I asked Grandma about him.

'Is Dill mad, Grandma? he seems it.'

She sat up stiffly.

'Everyone contains a seed of madness that makes them do strange things. With Dill, it's grown. It usually does after a personal tragedy,' she replied.

'What happened to him?' I asked.

'His mother died when he was very young. He's the youngest of eight boys. Petal was a great friend of mine. She was eighty when she had him. Tragic, it was. Dill's had a difficult childhood. The boys were good, they tried to help, but Sorrel found it hard to cope when they all left home, one after the other.'

Grandma's face clouded over and her eyes filled with tears. I gasped.

'Oh, how awful. But isn't eighty incredibly old to be having a baby?'

'Wood elves live longer than us. Sorrel's a hundred, but they can live to one hundred and eighty or even longer.'

'That's twice as long as humans. That means, in human years, Dill would be about fifteen, not much older than me.'

'Yes, I suppose it does,' answered Grandma.

'But why does he jump around all the time? It's like he's crazy.'

'He has wild mood swings, but he's very creative. Troubled children often are.'

Chapter

13

Sorrel's House

The next morning, I put on the new jeans and jumper Grandma had bought for me the day before. I was looking forward to seeing what the inside of an elf's house looked like.

We found Dill in the clearing outside his house, carving a huge tawny owl out of wood. His model was sat on a tree stump next to him. Perched on another trunk to the other side sat the raven I'd seen the day before. Something drew me towards it. 'You're beautiful,' I said, watching its black feathers shine, merging from midnight blue to iridescent green, like oil on water. It stared into my eyes and spoke.

'Call me when you need me and I'll find them for you.'

I jumped back, startled. Had it said, 'I'll find him for you.'

'What do you mean?' I asked it. Grandma turned round.

'What did you say?' she said. The raven took flight as she spoke. She ducked to avoid it, as it flew towards her and off into the woods. I watched it disappear, following its path through the trees. It was obvious no one else had heard the raven. I shook my head. I must be imagining things.

'Oh, nothing, Grandma,' I said, walking over towards Dill, who seemed to be in a trance, zoned out. Grandma coughed and Dill looked up. He opened a sack and took out a dead mouse which he threw to the owl.

As the owl gripped the mouse in its talons and flew off, Sorrel appeared.

'I'm so pleased you've come,' he said, taking my hand and clasping it tightly as Dill started to jump up and down, as if on an imaginary pogo stick.

'Come on in, I've made some of my special rabbit stew.' Sorrel gestured towards a little round green door which led to a house built deep into the hillside.

I had expected it to be dark inside because of the lack of windows, but it felt spacious and airy with high ceilings and daylight coming in through deep slits in the turf. Even though the furniture was all carved from wood, it felt modern, almost futuristic, not the type of house you'd expect to find dug into a hillside in a wood.

'Wow, it's lovely!' I said.

Sorrel beamed with pleasure, his big brown eyes brimming with pride.

'Yes, I built it myself with very basic tools and natural materials. We have everything we need here. We don't need taps as we have gravity-fed spring water, and thanks to Dill, we even have some solar panels. Got them off the Internet, he did.

Dill, why don't you show Noola your studio? Me and Isabel are going to have a natter and a glass of elderflower wine.'

Dill grabbed my arm and pulled me away, taking me up a spiral staircase to the first floor. At the top of the stairs, a circular landing had five doors leading off it. I remembered Grandma telling me that Dill had seven brothers; this house must have been full of life at one time. The fifth door was Dill's studio. On one side of the room was a desk with a computer and sound system. This side was tidy; it had plain white walls and shelves full of books lined up in neat rows, along with a family photo of Dill as a toddler, with seven other elves of different ages who all looked remarkably similar. On the other half of the room, the walls were painted black. Dill had set up a projector which cast images of red, blue and green lights onto the wall. They moved in a sequence of patterns before finishing in an explosion of fireworks and starting again. With clothes all over the floor and the bed unmade it looked like it belonged to an untidy teenager.

Dill sat down at his desk.

'Have a look round. There's a pile of phones in that drawer. Izzy said you don't have one. Take one and take a charger as well.'

I picked a bright green phone and showed it to Dill.

'Can I take this one?'

'Yeah, whichever you like. I'll show you how to use it later. I just need to check my emails. I've been waiting for someone to get back to me with a price for crocodile teeth.'

I pulled a face.

'Crocodile teeth.'

Dill laughed.

'Chillax, they don't pull them out while they're alive. They're taken from dead ones. Did ye know, crocodiles don't age. A seventy-year-old crocodile is as fit as a seven-year-old. They live till they're about eighty, then they die because they can't find enough food and because they've grown so big, they need masses of it. Don't tell Izzy, though. It's for a project of mine. Izzy likes to use plants in her remedies, most of the time, not animals, apart from the twerts, but they're not really either.'

'What are twerts, Dill?' I asked.

'They're hard to describe, horrible really. They're the souls of dead people; people who have done something bad or illegal. She finds them in the woods mostly, but sometimes she gets them from the fair. They have loads there. You can get some wicked ones.'

I gripped the back of Dill's chair.

Mammy had often told Uncle Ned that brewing spirits was illegal and if he got caught, he'd be put in jail for it. If he had…I couldn't bring myself to say the word or even think it, could he have been turned into a twert?

My voice quivered.

'Where does Grandma keep the twerts?' I asked him.

'In the room that leads off the cellar. She doesn't let anyone in that room, not even me, though I know she keeps the key on a hook in a cupboard under the sink.'

I decided to investigate the twerts at the first opportunity.

Dill settled down to read his emails while I looked round his room, still shaken. On a pin board I saw a poster. Attracted by the bright colours on it, I looked closer.

Underneath, attached by a pin, was a colourful yellow ticket.

I breathed heavily as though I'd been running. I couldn't move, and continued to stare at the poster. My only chance of finding Uncle Ned was getting to the Otherworld and the opportunity to get there was staring me in the face. That ticket suddenly made finding Uncle Ned feel possible.

Dill looked up from his computer screen and saw the look on my face.

'What's up?'

'You've got a t- ticket to the fair,' I managed to stutter.

'Yes, I go every year with Izzy. Next year we're looking for rare twerts. We need a vain one, and an addictive one; she can't find them in the woods.'

My mind whirled as fast as the lights flashing round the room.

'Can I go with you, Dill? I need to find my Uncle Ned. He was taken by the siseesh and I think he might be there.'

Dill shook his head.

'All the tickets for elves and pixies have gone. I looked on the website yesterday for a friend of mine. The only ones left are for witches and their apprentices.'

'Well, that's okay, I'll become a witch's apprentice,' I said.

Dill bounded across the room and started to jump up and down on his bed.

'You can't, it takes years. You'd never learn everything and pass the exams in time.' I gulped.

'Years?' I said, feeling the colour drain from my face.

'Yes, years. There's so much to learn,' said Dill.

'Well, what do you have to learn?' I asked, my voice high pitched and desperate.

Dill carried on bouncing.

'Well, hang on. There's a process. First of all, you need to be recommended.'

'By who?' I asked, knowing that Grandma would never recommend me. He stopped bouncing and stood with his hands on his hips.

'By the witch that wants you to be their apprentice, of course. That's the easy bit; it's just a letter to the witch's council . But then you'd have to master potion making. Now that's possible, what with you being of magic blood. You have to make three potions, two transforming and one affecting.'

'An affecting potion - is that a love philtre?' I asked, thinking of the bottles in Grandma's cellar.

'Yes, that's right. Affecting potions alter how people feel and transforming potions alter how people look.' He somersaulted off the bed, landing on the floor in front of me.

'But then you have to pass an online theory exam. That may be plausible, but it's probably impossible because you'd have to memorise all the books on your grandma's shelves and you've never even been to school.'

'Yes, but I can read; my Uncle Ned taught me,' I said, jutting out my chin.

'Well, even if you passed the exam, you'd still have to perform an example of transfiguration and that's definitely impossible.'

'What's transfiguration?' I asked, my voice now croaky with disappointment because of the lump that had appeared in my throat.

'That's the tricky bit. You have to turn someone,' Dill sat down on his bed and picked up a red juggling ball from his bedside cabinet,

'into something else,' he said, picking up a blue juggling ball and starting to juggle.

'I've been wanting to do it for years. I'm determined to turn the wood warden into a warthog but you need a voodoo amulet and they're impossible to get hold of. Believe me I've tried. So, I'd forget it, if I were you.'

He launched the balls into a basketball net on the back of his door, jumped on his bed and started to bounce again.

'There's always next time.'

I turned away from Dill and the flashing lights which were starting to make me feel dizzy. I put my hand into my coat pocket where the necklace from Juli Anabaluloo pulsed softly. I felt the serviette from Lula and took it out. The hair was still there. I smiled. I liked Lula. People as nice as her deserved to be happy. I began to devise a plan.

I could write the letter - and all the things I needed for potion making were in grandma's cellar. The recipes must be in there as well. I had the voodoo amulet from Juli in my pocket and I could still remember the words she'd chanted. As for the exam, Grandma had all the books I needed.

If getting to the fair was my only hope of finding Uncle Ned, and I had to become an apprentice witch to get there, I was going to do it. Nothing or no one was going to stop me.

Chapter
14

Beezlebag and the Twerts

Hi, Lula.' Grandma lowered her voice. She was in the kitchen on the phone but I could still hear.

'I was expecting it to be the social worker.'

'Oh, I shouldn't think they'll ring so soon. They're always so busy. It might be weeks before they get round to you but the child's no bother, is she?' said Lula.

'No, quite the opposite. She got up before me this morning, cleaned up, put the fire on and made her breakfast, then she made mine. Someone's trained her well.'

'Not like her mother then,' said Lula.

'No, her mother didn't move away from the television at her age, but I think she was about Noola's age when the trees started talking to her. It freaked her out. She became a near recluse, hardly ever went out after that, and when she did she met that awful Irish boy.' Grandma sighed.

'Anyway, it looks like she'll be staying a bit longer than I expected.' Relief flooded through me. But I needed to stay until the springtime, until I could find Uncle Ned.

Grandma's voice interrupted my thoughts.

'Anyway, I'll be round in a little while. We can talk about it then,' she said, putting down the phone and coming into the room where I pretended to be reading a book of spells.

'I'm going to Lula's for the evening. You can stay here with Buddy and Jonjo. Lock the door when I'm gone. That horrible man next door is always sneaking about.'

As soon as I was alone in the house, I decided to go and investigate the twerts. I found the key and was just about to enter the locked room when I heard the door upstairs open. I'd forgotten to lock the front door!

I hovered for a few moments, my skin prickling with fear, before hiding behind a stack of boxes.

A few moments later, I heard footsteps on the stairs and someone came in. I peered round the boxes and jumped in fright. Two metres away from me was Beezlebag.

Two bright red glowing eyes scanned the room. I stood still, hardly daring to breathe and tried to stifle an overwhelming urge to throw up. He started to rifle through the filing cabinet. Looking round again to make sure no one was there, he pulled out one of the files and started talking to himself.

'A hair from a blind unicorn ... a stray sod ... a mossy twert ... Where on earth am I going to find these things? It's impossible.' He quickly wrote the recipe down, then started to go through the boxes of ingredients.

'Aa ha,' he said as he found a box of unicorn hairs. For a few moments he disappeared out of sight but I could hear him opening jars and shuffling boxes, looking for the rest of the ingredients. Finally, he went into the room where grandma kept the twerts. I peeped through the keyhole to see for myself what they looked like.

The room was in darkness, so he flicked on the light.

Rows of cages, half covered in blankets, ran along the full length of the room. He pulled back the blankets and a look of horror flashed across his face. I held my breath and shut my eyes, terrified of what I was about to see and frightened to make a noise in case I was discovered.

I opened my eyes and froze.

In the cages were the most hideous-looking creatures I had ever seen. Turning the light on had woken them up and they started to hurl abuse at him.

'Wot you doing in 'ere, you bald-headed freak?' shouted one. It was green and slimy and looked like a clump of wet moss with a face. But not a nice face, a terrifying face, a face that would give you nightmares. It pulled a huge green bogey out of its nose and flicked it at him. Beezlebag stood paralysed, too frightened to move. The label dangling from the cage said: **MOSSY TWERT (GREEDY)**

Next to the mossy twert was a cage with what looked like a stone the size of a small turnip in it. The "stone" started to make clicking noises with its tongue. Its eyes met with a squint in the middle and it had a hooked nose arching over bulbous dribbling lips. The stone stared at Beezlebag with an evil look in one of its eyes; the other seemed to be staring at the door.

'As that old witch sent you to do 'er dirty work, you goggle-eyed gargoyle? Well, don't think yer pickling me. Just try it and see wot 'appens,' said the stone. The label on the cage said: **STONY TWERT (CANTANKEROUS)**

From the next cage, a huge rotting mushroom stared out with a vacant expression. Half of its face was missing - eaten away. The rest was decaying round the edges. It scratched itself with long mouldy fingers, sending plumes of spores flying round the room. **FUNGAL TWERT** said its label.

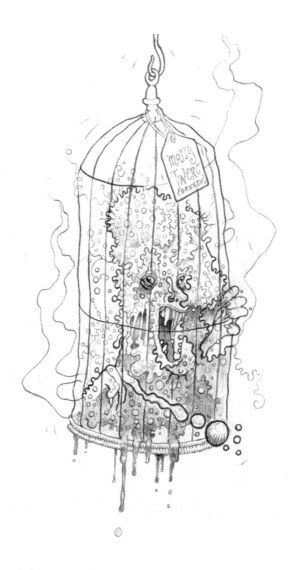

Beezlebag started to scratch himself all over. I watched through the keyhole as he threw a blanket over the cages and turned towards the door. He stopped dead, staring up at something, but I couldn't see what it was. After a few moments, he picked up some jars from a shelf in front of him and darted for the door.

As Beezlebag hurried out of the cellar and ran upstairs to the bathroom, I ducked down behind a stack of boxes. I tiptoed after him, shaken by the sight of the horrible creatures in the cages. I looked through the keyhole to see him hunched over the sink looking in the mirror. His face had turned pale and something was wriggling across it. It looked like the bogey was burrowing its way into his cheek.

He seemed to be shaking as he grabbed the handle of the bathroom cabinet, almost pulling it off its hinges. He found some tweezers and pulled at the thing on his face. The thing that started out as a slimy green bogey, flicked at him from the disgusting mossy twert, was now coming out of his cheek and it was at least seven centimetres long. The bug had left a small bleeding hole. He stopped the blood with some toilet paper, leaned over the sink and threw up.

I tiptoed into my bedroom and a few moments later, Beezlebag ran down the stairs and out of the house.

Sitting on my bed, I tried to take in what I'd just seen. Grandma needed to know about Beezlebag but I couldn't be the one to tell her. She'd be straight on the phone to the social workers if she found out I'd l hadn't locked the door and Beezlebag had been in the cellar. But one thing I was sure about, Uncle Ned could never, never, ever, even if he had done something illegal, have ended up as a twert.

Chapter

15

Schooldays

A week after arriving at Grandma's I started at Pebble Bridge Primary School, a large stone building almost entirely hidden behind glossy green ivy. It was like an old, haunted house from a Dracula movie. My stomach had been churning since I woke up this morning. Now it was threatening to relieve its contents all over the headmaster, Mr Plunkett, who stood waiting at the school gates.

Ten minutes later, we stood in his office where he summoned my teacher, Miss Newt. I looked up at the woman towering over me. Her small beady eyes were hidden behind very large horn-rimmed spectacles. She was dressed in a black skirt and jumper and over her narrow, sloping shoulders hung a thick black cloak.

She lifted her shoulders and lowered her neck, surveying me up and down, looking like a very large bird of prey about to eat a very small mouse.

I shuddered as the late summer sun streaming through the window opposite cast the shadow of a giant vulture on the wall. My teacher looked far from pleased.

'Go stand outside Noola.'

I stood outside, peeped through the window and listened.

'I can't have an eleven-year-old in my class who's never been to school,' she said to the headmaster.

'What will that do for my Ofsted results? She'll bring all my averages down.'

Mr Plunkett folded his arms.

'Listen, Vanessa, the child's got off to a bad start. She's been abandoned by her parents, but her grandmother assures me she's very bright. She'll soon catch up. Not everyone has had the benefit of a privileged upbringing like yours.'

'I'll give her six months. I'm sick of teaching half-breeds and dummies. If she hasn't caught up by then, she'll have to go down a year.' The teacher stomped out of the office and I had to jog to keep up with her all the way to the classroom.

The morning flew by. I had wanted to go to school for as long as I could remember. I was so happy to be there, I listened, I was polite, I was so keen to learn I consumed every bit of information, registered it, digested it, and it stuck. I had never realised it before, but I had an extraordinary memory.

At playtime I sat on the playground wall watching the children play, not daring to approach them after my experience with the boys from Cork.

I saw a boy with a shock of black hair and dark bushy eyebrows walking round the playground with two others. He was looking for someone to pick on and he was heading my way. He stood in front of me with his hands on his hips.

'Eeh, look wot wi got 'ere, Roland. It's a frizzy freak, a ginger geek. It's the witch's kid.' I jumped down from the wall and glared at him. My first thought was that he bore a definite similarity to an orangutan. His oval head, was perched on top of enormous shoulders from which hung two long hairy arms. From Grandma's description, it could only be Rodney Gobbit.

His friend grinned, revealing two long pointed front teeth which made him look like a rat in a school uniform - with glasses. The other boy, who had long blond hair and vivid

blue eyes, shuffled from one foot to another, looking uncomfortable.

Rodney grabbed hold of my hair and lifted me off my feet until his huge face was inches from mine.

'Don't be trying any o' that hocus pocus on us, kid.'

I kicked him in the shins as hard as I could until he let go.

Rodney turned to the blond boy.

'Ere, Fred, catch 'old o' that skinny carrot stick so I can teach 'er a lesson.'

'Leave 'er alone, Rodney. She ain't done nuffin to you,' he replied.

'Not yet she an't, but she's a witch an ye don't see wot they're gonna do cos they're sly. They make dolls that look like you an' stick pins in 'em. They twiddle their ears an' turn yer into frogs and stuff. She's got massive ears.'

I stood with my hands on my hips, defiant.

'It's my Grandma who's the witch. I'm going to tell her to turn you into a slug and when she does, I'm going to squish you.' I wriggled my foot as if I was squashing something.

'Well, don't ye know we burn witches raand 'ere, so jus' let 'er try it,' replied Rodney.

'Yeah,' said Roland, tottering behind. 'We fry 'em like a fritter. We smoke 'em like a kipper.' His small shifty eyes gleamed with delight as Rodney grabbed my hair again and started to drag me round the playground. Fred skulked away, distancing himself from the other boys and I as I tried to kick

Rodney again, two pigeons who had been sitting on the bike shed roof, swooped down on him, splattering him with poo. He suddenly let go. My eyes watered and my head stung.

'Serves you right, you great big baboon,' I said, as Rodney frantically tried to get the pigeon poo out of his eyes.

The teacher, hearing the commotion, came out into the playground.

'Get in here this minute, Rodney Gobbit,' she said, grabbing his ear and marching him inside.

I bit my trembling lower lip to stop myself from crying and saw the wood pigeons returning to the bike shed. I ran over and jumped onto a low wall behind it so I was at eye level with them.

'Hawarye? I'm Noola. Thanks for sticking up for me,' I said to a rather fat old pigeon, who was busy pecking a mouldy Jammie Dodger.

'No problem, lass. Aam Syd, an' this 'ere is me mate, Charlie. Pleased to meet you, too. Ye looked to be 'avin' a spot o' bother wi' that big gonk,' said the pigeon.

'I'm not scared of him. Soon I'm going to be a witch like my grandma, then he'd better watch out,' I replied.

'My, yer a feisty one fer a fledgling. Well, if ye want us to splat 'im again, just give us the nod. It'ud give us great pleasure. 'E's a nasty piece o' work that one. We'll be keeping a close eye on 'im,' said Syd.

'Thanks,' I said.

The bell rang for the end of playtime and the birds flew off.

That evening, while we were having supper, I asked Grandma, 'Is it true that they burn witches round here?'

'They used to,' she replied, 'but now people are a lot more civilised. Being a witch is a good profession. They do good things for good people.'

I mulled this over and had an idea.

'Grandma, if witches do good things for good people, does that mean they can do bad things to bad people?'

She shuffled uncomfortably in her chair.

'I tried to turn Beezlebag next door into a chicken once. He grew feathers out of his head instead of hair for a while, until he shaved it. Now he keeps trying to steal my hair-growing recipe because it won't grow back. As I said before, transfiguration isn't my strong point. So, the answer is yes, I suppose they can.'

My whole face went hot and I closed my eyes tightly. Now I understood why Beezlebag had been in the cellar.

'Bad things for bad people,' I whispered. I would concentrate on Rodney Gobbit first and worry about Beezlebag later.

It took me a few minutes before I trusted myself to speak without my voice sounding shaky. I looked out of the window so Grandma couldn't see the guilty look on my face.

'Grandma, what sort of potion is a hair-growing potion?'

'It's a transforming potion. Remedy 49 for hair growth, 50 for hair removal - different ingredients, different results. You can't get either in the shops. They're my best selling line. That's why there's no bald people in Pebble Bridge. Dr Dunderfield's my best customer for Remedy 49. Why all the questions?'

'Oh, nothing, Grandma. I'm just interested, that's all.'

Grandma smiled, she seemed pleased.

'Well, it's good that you're interested. Your Mammy never was - quite the opposite, in fact. Get off to bed now and I'll see you in the morning.'

In bed, I thought things through. I needed to make two transforming potions and one affecting potion. I considered asking Grandma for help - she'd been happy that I'd asked about her work - but she might say no and then she'd know what I was up to and she'd be on her guard and watching me.

My only hope of finding Uncle Ned was to get to the Otherworld and my only hope of getting there was to be a witch's apprentice so I couldn't risk telling Grandma. I decided on a plan. If it worked, it would be a suitable punishment for that horrible Rodney Gobbit and also help towards my witch's apprenticeship.

Chapter
16

Noola's revenge

I stared out of the window, watching the steep valley sides stretch into the distance like a long dark tunnel, when something whistled past my ear. I turned round to see Rodney Gobbit disappearing behind his desk lid as Miss Newt walked in.

'Okay class, listen very carefully. This term's project is about the environment. Now, you've all heard about climate change and the damaging effects it's going to have on your future. So I want you all to write a statement about what you think you could do to help. For the next few months, I want you to talk to people and do your research. There will be a prize for the person who comes up with the best answer.'

'Ouch,' I said. This time, the something had stung. I turned round to see Rodney with a broad grin plastered across his face and a catapult in his hand.

'Are you listening Fionnuala?'

'Yes, Miss,' I said, rubbing my cheek and sighing. The last thing I needed with all the work I had to do was a school project about the environment.

Out in the playground, I watched, as the other kids ran about laughing and joking, or checking their phones, and I realised how it felt to be totally invisible. Until I saw Rodney and his sidekick, Roland, approaching in the distance and wished I was.

This time though, I was more prepared.

'A thought a told you witches aren't welcome raand eer,' he said, picking me up by my hair. I reached up, digging my fingers into his scalp and pulled his hair as hard as I could.

Rodney squealed like a wounded pig and started to swing me round as the other children scrambled to get out of the way. I let go and moments later, there was a rush of wings from above. It was Charlie the pigeon.

'Bombs away,' he shouted, swooping down on Rodney and splattering him with poo.

'Bang on target,' shouted Syd, following close behind. Enemy in sight; going in.' He swooped low, unleashing a barrage of pigeon poo over the howling Rodney.

'Take that, bully boy.' The birds carried on until Rodney looked like a tin of paint had been tipped over him.

'Mission accomplished,' shouted Charlie as he flew off back to the bike shed.

'I'm off to refuel,' shouted Syd, flying off towards the park.

I ran past the other children to the cloakroom where I wrapped Rodney's hair in a tissue and put it in my coat pocket. The shrieks and shouting from the playground turned to laughter and through the window I could see Rodney glued to the spot and quivering like a giant white blancmange.

That night, after Grandma had gone to bed, I took the keys and went down to the dimly lit cellar. In the filing cabinet, all the remedies were filed neatly in alphabetical order.

I took out the recipes for the hair-growing remedy and the love philtre. Grandma's handwriting was spidery and difficult to read in the dim light so I picked up one of the glowing jars from the shelf above to use as a torch.

FAIRIES' WINGS read the label. On the back of the jar it said, "Highly effective and very toxic. Only to be used by those who possess the proper talent."

Putting the jar close to the book, I read the recipe.

Love Philtre

1. A teaspoon of ground Sea serpent bones
2. A teaspoon of dried hogthistle
3. A simpering twert
4. A hair from the person looking for love

I set to work, instinctively knowing what to do. As I worked, the remedies on the shelves started to glow, lighting up the ceiling and making it easier to see. The ingredients were easy to find as they also were neatly labelled in alphabetical order.

As I took the lid off the jar containing the ground sea serpent bones, a familiar smell wafted from it and the brackish smell of the sea transported me back home to Ballybay. A picture of Uncle Ned lying on the beach flashed into my head, making me sway and almost drop the jar. I shook my head, pushing the thoughts away and put a teaspoonful into the blender, followed by a teaspoon of dried hogthistle.

After mixing these together I moved on to the hair growing remedy. This recipe seemed much more complicated.

A hair from a blind unicorn
A fairy wing
A stray sod
A mossy twert
A hair from the customer

As I put the hair from the blind unicorn into the blender, it suddenly struck me that a few weeks ago I knew nothing of this magical world and now here I was brewing a potion with a hair from a blind unicorn in it. I wondered what Uncle Ned would make of it all and longed for my old life back. I shivered, becoming suddenly aware of the door behind me and what was behind it. My medallion glowed, giving me courage and reminding me why I was there. I opened the jar containing the fairy wings.

As I took the lid off, the petals quivered as if they were alive. I felt a strange sense of déjà vu. There was something familiar about these flowers, something I couldn't quite put my finger on. Taking one out, a tingling sensation rippled through my fingers, up my arm and neck and into my head. All my senses became heightened. Feeling suddenly queasy, I dropped the petal into the blender. Now all I needed was the stray sod, the mossy twert and the hair from Rodney.

After a few minutes searching for the stray sods, I came across some fish tanks without water but with small clumps of grass in them.

BABY STRAY SODS HANDLE WITH CARE

said a sticker on the front of the tank. I took the lid off and reached in to pick one up. As I grabbed it, the others started to jump about. I looked closely at the one in my hand and discovered that the grass was only a camouflage. Underneath the grass was a tiny creature with a face, arms and legs and two out-of-proportion, large front teeth which it sank into my finger as it squirmed to escape.

As it wriggled and writhed, I gripped it tighter and read the instructions under the recipe.

'Place the stray sod in hot water before use.' I turned on the hot tap and ducked the wriggling sod underneath it. It wilted like spinach and shrank to half its size. I quickly put it into the second blender with the other ingredients before adding the hair from Rodney.

So far, so good. Now all I needed were the twerts, but they were in the other room behind that door and I was too frightened to go in. I steeled myself. There was no other way. I took the key out of my pocket and opened the door quietly, taking care not to wake the twerts in the cages. I looked up at the shelves that had stopped Beezlebag in his tracks, and froze, realising now why he'd looked so terrified.

Lined up on the shelves were rows of glass bell jars containing heads floating in some sort of liquid. I wanted to run but I stood mesmerised.

In the first jars, the faces were grotesque. Some looked like they were screaming; some of them looked angry; but they all had the chilling look of people who had done terrible things. The next row of jars had a sign saying **PICKLED TWERTS WEEK 2**. The expressions on their faces had changed. They had dull lifeless eyes, flabby chinless faces and thin, bloodless lips.

Now I realised why the twerts in the cages were so angry - this was to be their fate. On the third row were jars full of slimy water. The labels read **PERFECTLY PICKLED TWERTS**. Below the bell jars with the gruesome heads were all the various pickled twerts in small individual jars, labelled according to the particular twert they had in them. I found the jars I needed and left the room.

I worked quickly. Thinking of Uncle Ned kept me going, and I had my appointment for my booster with the doctor tomorrow. I added the hair from Lula to the love philtre. It dissolved straight away. Then I added some bogglestrop berries to the two potions. This wasn't in the recipe but I thought it might liven things up. I put the tops back on and put them in my pocket. As I finished, I heard Grandma moving about upstairs, so I slipped quietly back to my bedroom.

There, I put a little bit of each potion into a separate bottle to send away to the witches' council, and hid them in a drawer. I sat down and wrote the letter of recommendation, signing Grandma's name by copying it from a letter I'd found in the cellar with her signature on. I'd have to hijack the post for the next few weeks in case they needed to consult with her.

When everything was quiet again, I tiptoed downstairs where the Gobbits' hair-removing remedy was waiting for collection and switched the bottles.

I arrived at the doctor's with Lula, feeling particularly pleased with myself. I couldn't take my eyes off him as he bustled round the surgery. His thick black shiny hair was tied in a ponytail and he looked like he'd had a spray tan. Lula had gone all giggly and was acting like a teenager with a crush.

'Could you put my name down for one of those gastric bands, doctor? I just can't seem to shift this weight. Every time I go on a diet, I seem to put on more,' she said.

Dr Dunderfield looked at Lula like she was five years old.

'Lula, dear,' he sighed, 'if you stopped eating half the contents of your café, you'd lose weight. You don't need a gastric band, you need willpower, and I can't give you a prescription for that.'

Lula turned a bright shade of purple. Neither of them noticed as I tipped the love philtre into the jug of blueberry juice he kept on his desk.

Coming out of the doctor's surgery, Lula fumed.

'How could I have ever considered going out with that man? He's an arrogant, pompous pig – your grandma was right. Never mind, one day I'll get my own back on him, you just wait.' I gulped. What had I done? Maybe the love philtre wouldn't work.

That evening, Bob Gobbit came to collect the special hair-removing remedy, and the following week Rodney came to school wearing a baseball hat pulled down over his face.

I watched him as he skulked past his friends, avoiding their curious stares. Suddenly, he let off a large paaarp! The force of the blast propelled him six metres, face forward, onto the ground. He got up, took off his cap and wiped his forehead with the back of his hand. I turned away so he couldn't see me laughing. His hair had started growing down his forehead and onto his ears.

'Look, Rodney's turning into a rabbit,' shouted Roland, as Rodney let off another blast of wind, pitching him forward. The playground exploded with laughter as Rodney got up, ran out of the playground and off down the road.

The following Friday teatime, Liberty Gobbit arrived to see Grandma.

'Oh, Isabel!' she cried. 'Whats happened? The remedy hasn't worked and Rodney won't go out of the house. He's farting like a carthorse, and the stench is vile – he's making our lives a misery. He's going crazy, he looks like a monkey, and he keeps saying he's been cursed.'

Grandma got out her handkerchief and wiped her face.

'I made the remedy as I usually do. I don't know what could have happened.' I looked up from my plate to see her staring straight at me. I looked away and started to chew my food slowly to stop myself from smiling. She turned to Liberty. 'I'll go and get some more, but could you please ask Rodney to stop picking on Noola. It could be the reason why the remedy hasn't worked this time.' She came back from the cellar with two bottles. 'This one's for the wind problem. Tell him to stay by the toilet after he's drunk it, just in case.'

Chapter

17

November
Katy Clapshot

It was a clear, crisp winter's day. I sat on the playground wall watching the other children and thinking things through. I had been at school for four weeks now and still hadn't made any friends. Uncle Ned had said I was different, and kids don't like other kids who are different, but lots of these kids were different. Elsie had a hump on her back and Ethan had a funny eye. But that makes you special, being different, doesn't it? Uncle Ned had said so.

I watched them as they played happily together. Maybe they wouldn't play with me because my grandma was a witch.

I ran my fingers over the picture on the cover of the book I was reading. It was a book on wildflowers and their uses in medicine called Potions, Lotions and Magical Transformations. It had a picture of a flower on it called a Fringed Polygala Paucifolia, better known as 'fairy wings', the same flower I'd used in Rodney Gobbit's hair-growing remedy. As my fingers ran over the hot pink fairy wings' flower, they began to tingle.

'I wish I had a friend,' I said, 'then maybe I wouldn't feel so sad and lonely.' A few moments later, I was interrupted by someone.

'What's that your reading?' said the girl.

I recognised her. She was from London and had started school that day. Short and top heavy, with huge buck teeth, she was called Katy Clapshot.

'It's a book on wildflowers, so it is.'

'Your'e odd-looking,' said Katy.

'Well, you wouldn't exactly win the Rose of Tralee,' I replied.

'What's the Rose of Tralee?' said Katy.

'It's a beauty competition for empty-headed bimbos watched by empty-headed oafs, my mammy says,' I said, jumping down from the wall. Katy scowled.

'When I grow up, I'm going to get my teeth fixed, then I'm going to America to be a famous actress and singer.'

'My Uncle Ned wants to go to America,' I said, my voice wavering.

'To be an actor?' asked Katy.

'To see the Statue of Liberty and eat shrimps.'

'What are you going to be when you grow up?' asked Katy.

'I'm going to be a famous hedgewitch, like my grandma.'

'OMG, what does a hedgewitch do?' gasped Katy.

'They do good things for good people and bad things to bad people.'

Katy was quiet for a moment, taking this in, before she spoke again.

'I wear a 34 Double D bra,' she said, sticking her chest out with a smug look on her face.

'I can understand what birds are saying,' I said, pushing back my shoulders and searching Katy's face for a glimmer of amazement. Katy seemed unimpressed.

'Did your granny make your hair curly?' she asked.

'No, it's natural. I was born with a head of curly hair,' I said.

'I have to have curlers put in mine, but most days my mum never has the time, what with the baby and her new boyfriend.'

'Do you like nature?' I asked.

'Not really,' replied Katy. 'Could your granny make my hair curly?'

'Yes, probably. She has remedies for most things.'

'If you ask her, I'll play with you, if you like. It doesn't look like you've got many friends.'

The bell rang. Playtime was over and the conversation ended.

I ran home from school that afternoon. If I could make Katy a remedy to make her hair curly, I would have made the two transforming potions I needed for my apprenticeship, and perhaps I would have a friend. I flew through the door to find Dill bounding round the office with a fishing net. The desiccated scuttlebugs had arrived and they were far from desiccated.

Dozens of the bugs were scuttling round the office. They were like giant neon ladybirds. As soon as Dill got near one, it took flight. One of them hovered above me.

'Get out of the way,' he screamed, heading towards it with a fishing net. The sight of Dill frightened it so much, it dropped a lump of gloopy neon-coloured poo.

Dill jumped over the furniture, screaming with excitement as he launched himself at the unfortunate bugs who performed acrobatics, circling the room trying to avoid him.

I escaped into the living room where Buddy was watching the news. 'Where's Grandma?' I asked him.

He smiled. 'She's in the garden. There's been a right to-do. She said she's staying out there until Dill catches those bugs.' He chuckled again.

'Which could take hours.' Buddy relished a drama.

I went into the kitchen, shutting the door and made my way down to the cellar. If Grandma was going to be in the garden for hours, I should have time to make Katy's hair-curling potion. I reached the cellar and turned the handle but it wouldn't open. It was locked! Grandma must suspect I'd been in there. I weighed up my options: I could look for the key, which could be hidden anywhere, or I could ask for her help. Remembering Grandma wasn't in a very good mood, I decided to try to find the key first. I went upstairs and searched everywhere I could think she might have put it with no success. I sat on my bed and thought things through. I had to make the third potion to have any chance of going to the fair. Grandma had been much friendlier recently and she didn't need to know about the others. There was nothing else for it.

In the garden, Grandma was savagely pulling dead weeds out of her vegetable patch.

'That boy, I don't know what's going to become of him, I really don't. He's done it on purpose, I'm sure he has.' She threw the trowel into her bucket and moved on to the next row.

'I can't send them back. Goodness knows how they survived the journey this far, but I can't set them free either. I'll have to put up a greenhouse to keep them in. I could kill him sometimes.'

I steeled myself.

'Grandma, could you show me how to make a remedy for a girl at school to make her hair curly. She said if I do, she might be my friend.'

Grandma looked up at me and frowned. 'Noola, why would you want to be friends with someone so shallow? Surely, if she's worth having as a friend, she wouldn't put conditions in the way.'

'Please, Grandma, please. I've never had a friend,' I begged. Grandma sighed.

'Yes, okay, I will, but don't make a habit of this. My remedies are expensive.' I ran to hug her at the same moment as the gloopy poo started to trickle down my face.

Grandma pushed me away, 'What the ... what's that?' she said, wiping the gloopy substance with a handkerchief. 'Your freckles are disappearing,' she said, rubbing my face, erasing the rest of them.

'Oh, I think one of those bugs must have pooed on my head,' I said. Grandma smiled.

'Go wash your face,' she said, pushing past me and into the house.

'I need to help Dill catch the scuttlebugs.'

That evening, after tea, we went down to the cellar.

'Right,' said Grandma going to the filing cabinet, 'in here are all my recipes. They're in alphabetical order so you need to look for H for hair.' She was watching me closely to see my reactions. I tried to look as if I hadn't seen any of it before. I opened the cabinet and read the subheadings under hair.

Hair removing

Hair growing

Hair curling

I pulled the hair-curling recipe out and read the ingredients.

A hair from a screech owl's toe

The flower of a dog's tooth violet

The root from a curly Kale

A biddles piddle

'What's a biddles piddle?' I asked.

'Don't ask,' she said.

'Now, all the ingredients are in these boxes. They're filed in alphabetical order to make them easier to find.' I found the ingredients easily and put them on the table. Grandma stood with her arms folded, watching me intently.

'Good. Now, under the list of the ingredients are the instructions. Take your time and keep checking them. I'll watch you.'

I made the potion in five minutes flat.

'Well done, Noola. That was extraordinary,' she said.

After I'd gone to bed, I heard her on the phone. I stood at the top of the stairs and listened.

'It was extraordinary, Lula. She's a natural.'

'Well, why don't you make her your apprentice?'

'I've told you why.' She'll end up leaving me like the rest of them. Or her uncle will turn up and take her away. She's a good kid and I like her company but it won't last. It never does.'

I got back in bed and thought about what she'd said. I wished more than anything in the world that Uncle Ned would turn up and take me home.

A few days later, I took the hair-curling remedy to school and the day after, Katy came to school with a head of curly hair. She strutted around the playground looking like a freshly groomed labradoodle.

'Wow, you look nice,' I said.

'Yes, and all thanks to you. You look nice too. What happened to your freckles?'

I didn't think it was the right time to mention the scuttlebug poo.

'My grandma got rid of them,' I said.

'Would you like to be my friend?' asked Katy. I felt a warm glow inside. I had made three potions now; I was well on my way to becoming a witch's apprentice and finding Uncle Ned, and, I had made a friend at last.

We wandered round the playground, arm in arm.

Even Rodney Gobbit left us alone; I think he'd learnt his lesson about picking on me, and he seemed quite taken with Katy and her 34 double D chest.

That evening, I ran home from school and into my bedroom. I got out my notebook, ripped out my bucket list and rewrote it.

GO TO SCHOOL ✓
MAKE A FRIEND ✓
FIND UNCLE NED
BE A WITCH LIKE GRANDMA

Chapter
18

December
Buddy meets Dr Dunderfield

With Christmas approaching, the weather had turned very cold. I was sat in the living room reading a book about the use of trees in medicine, with Buddy reading it over my shoulder.

'Did you know, Noola, that a quarter of all medicines contain chemicals found in trees, and that every minute an area of trees the size of a football pitch is lost as forests are cleared for farmland or harvested to make timber and palm oil? It seems the human population is trying to annihilate itself. When the trees are gone, where will they get their medicine from then?' he said.

'Would you test me? I think I know a lot of them.'

Buddy's mouth dropped open.

'Well, I am impressed. I thought you were one sandwich short of a picnic, what with you never having been to school. That's incredible.'

The door opened and Katy bounced into the room.

'Hi, Noola, I've brought some stuff to make Christmas decorations.'

She saw Buddy and let out a small squeak.

'Oh, it's awake,' she said.

'I'm not an IT, I'm a tree,' said Buddy.

'Do you know, young lady, that the future health and welfare of humanity will be determined to a great extent by the rainforests, and do you know that that means TREES? I'd advise you to have a little respect.'

Katy walked backwards until she reached the wall. Slithering slowly onto the floor, she sat there glowering at Buddy.

'Here, read this,' I said, thrusting the book into Buddy's twiggy hands to distract him.

'It can read,' whispered Katy … I nodded.

'And he knows how to work the internet. Grandma's assistant, Dillon, gave him his old computer.'

As we sat on the floor making paper chains, there was a knock on the door. Grandma came up from the cellar with a crate of boxes and answered it.

'Come in,' she said, leading Dr Dunderfield into the room where Buddy was flicking through the pages of my book. The doctor caught sight of him and jumped behind Grandma.

'Don't worry about Buddy, he's harmless,' said Grandma.

'Go sit down. I've got your remedies ready. I'm making some tea - would you like some?'

'Err, yes, that would be nice,' said the doctor, sitting down on the sofa opposite Buddy, who cleared his throat.

'So, you're the doctor, I presume.'

'Err, yes, yes. Pleased to meet you. I've heard a lot about you,' the doctor answered.

'Did you know that we trees are the lungs of this planet, and that an average-sized tree produces enough oxygen to keep a family of four breathing?'

'Well, of course I know that trees are very important to the environment. We couldn't live without you.'

'Well, I would imagine you're quite influential, being a doctor, wouldn't you say?' said Buddy.

'Well, err, s-sort of,' said the doctor. Who would you like me to influence?'

'Tell the council to forget about that new retail park in town, opposite the health centre. Leave it as a park. Green places relax people, lower heart rates and reduce stress,' said Buddy, loving his new audience. 'The council are a load of halfwits, baboons, imbeciles. Someone needs to make them see sense.'

'I'm afraid the plans have been passed. I don't think they'd listen to me at this stage.' said the doctor.

Buddy started to shout. 'There'll be more floods, droughts and forest fires. The Amazon is burning as we speak. You humans need to change the way you live. Trees recycle carbon dioxide. Plant more, stop chopping them down. I wish I had my roots back, I'd walk to Downing Street. I'd make them listen.' Jonjo started to flap his wings.

'Get me out, get me out! It's the end of the world! We're all doomed!' he squawked.

The doctor sat, open mouthed, as Buddy continued.

'And what do you think about Global warming?'

'Well, errr, it is, err, getting warmer. In fact, my mother and I went to Devon, it was like being-'

'Well, I'll tell you what I think,' interrupted Buddy.

'It all started with Global warming, then it became climate change, now it's a climate crisis. Apparently, the scientists have been banging on about it for thirty years.

'Well, I say, THEY DIDN'T SHOUT LOUD ENOUGH, and now they're trying to invent great carbon-guzzling machines to deal with the problem.

'Well, ye know what? ITS TOO LATE. And besides, don't they know the most efficient carbon guzzling machines have been around for thousands of years? They're called TREES. So why don't you humans plant more and stop chopping them down?'

The doctor shuffled as if he had bugs in his trousers as Grandma came in with a tray of tea and biscuits.

As she poured the tea, a loud paarrrp reverberated round the room. It came from the doctor and was so strong it lifted him off the sofa, setting me and Katy into a fit of giggles. Grandma looked shocked as the doctor wiped his face with a handkerchief. Jonjo flapped his wings in alarm.

'It's starting. The world's ending. There's been an explosion!' he squawked. I opened the cage and took Jonjo out, stroking his head to soothe him. He buried his head into my armpit and hid.

'Did you also know, doctor,' continued Buddy sternly 'that trees absorb odours and pollutant gases?'

'Oh, shut up, Buddy,' said Grandma.

'Nigel doesn't want a lecture on the physiology of trees.'

'Sorry, Isabel,' the doctor said, his face as red as a ripe tomato.

'I've had this problem for weeks now. I've tried everything, but I can't seem to get rid of it. It's so embarrassing. It even happens in the surgery. I've had to start playing background music and turning it up when I feel one coming on.'

I remembered the bogglestrop berries. I'd only put a teaspoon in the love philtre.

'Hang on, Nigel. I have something to sort it out,' said Grandma. She went downstairs and came back with another bottle of the amber-coloured liquid. 'Drink this, then go home and stay by the toilet. You should be okay in a couple of hours.' The doctor drank the liquid and got up to go.

As he was leaving, he hesitated at the door and turned around.

'Isabel, you couldn't put a good word in for me with Lula, could you? She seemed so keen to go on a date with me, but now she's not answering my calls and I can't stop thinking about her.' Grandma looked astonished while I froze.

The love philtre had worked!

'Yes, I'll speak to her,' said Grandma, narrowing her eyes and casting me a sideways glance. 'You know Lula, she's probably just lost her phone.'

Half an hour after the doctor and Katy had gone, Jonjo was still shaking. I sat with him on my lap, stroking him. I lifted him up and whispered to him.

'I know how you feel, Jonjo. I'm missing my Uncle Ned. We've both lost the one we love most in the world. If you tell me what happened to Juno, I might be able to help you find her.' Jonjo gazed up at me, nestled his head into my chest and fell asleep.

Settling him back in his cage, I went upstairs. My notebook was open at my bucket list. I picked up a pen and added FIND JUNO.

Getting ready for bed, I smiled. It had been a very productive day. I got out the three small bottles and wrapped them in brown paper. Then I looked up the address I needed from the witches' web and wrote out a label. I would post them off in the morning before school.

Chapter
19

March
Beezlebag

Even though Grandma had stopped mentioning social workers and foster parents, finding Uncle Ned was never far from my thoughts. The fair was only weeks away and I was well on my way to becoming a witch's apprentice.

A month after posting the potions away, I woke to the sound of the letterbox rattling.

'Post.' Shouted Buddy.

I jumped out of bed and ran downstairs before Grandma got there first. Two letters lay on the mat, one addressed to Grandma with an official looking stamp had WITCHES' COUNCIL written in the corner. The other was a packet of seeds I'd ordered off the Internet.

'Anything for me?' shouted Grandma from the kitchen.

'No, just some seeds,' I shouted, running upstairs. I pulled out the letter and read it.

For the attention of Isabel Flynn:

Dear Isabel

We wish to inform you that all of the
potions presented by your apprentice,
Noola O'Brien, exceed the statutory
level of achievement grade one.
Noola is making excellent progress.
Please send proof of transfiguration
and complete the online theory exam
by the closing date 19.3.19

Best regards
Meliza Mystic
Witches' Council
Pendle

I sat down on my bed, relief flooding through me.

All I needed to do now was some transfiguration and
my theory exam. My emotions changed from exhilaration
to despair. I longed to see Uncle Ned again but what if he
wasn't there?

It had been four months since the sun had ventured over
the steep sides of the valley. Used to the wide-open spaces
and luminosity of the seaside, I was beginning to think
Pebble Bridge must be the gloomiest place in the world, but
today when I looked out of the window, the sky had turned
blue, and everything looked different.

I had sown some seeds that I'd ordered off the Internet
called Gurglegit seeds which could be used in transfiguration
spells. Pleased with my interest in plants, Grandma had

started giving me a small allowance to pay for them. It said on the instructions that if you managed to get your victim to eat four of the seeds from the fruit of the plant, you were 100% sure of success. With only weeks until the fair, I was getting anxious. I needed to practise.

I had put the seeds on trays on the windowsill and tended to them every day and now they were big enough to plant out.

After breakfast, I ventured into the garden. A long stone wall ran down one side. On its other side, a steep drop led to the towpath bordering the canal which was very still and quiet, not like the sea. At the bottom of the garden, over the canal, an ancient stone bridge led to the woods. Grandma had told me stories of when the canal was used for carrying freight, and the narrowboats were pulled by horses. A narrowboat chugged slowly past. These days they usually carried tourists who hired them for the weekend.

I walked round the garden. It had a wild overgrown look and it was coming alive. All around, little points were appearing out of the damp earth, and the apple and cherry blossoms were coming into bud. On the dull grey branches of the trees, leaves were unfurling, sprouting tufts of vibrant green. There were birds twittering and singing from every bush and tree, and the grass seemed to have grown overnight. Spring had arrived at last.

I found the perfect place at the bottom of the garden to plant out my seedlings - beneath the tall green fence. It was the only bare space available and it never occurred to me that there might be a reason for this. As I dug a hole, I felt a trickle of something wet coming from above. I looked up and jumped with fright; the beginnings of a scream swelling in my throat. Hanging over the fence with a watering can in his hand was Beezlebag.

His once bald head was now covered in long bushy grey hair. I gasped. He had managed to make the hair-growing remedy! Small, red, hooded eyes leered at me. His cruel mouth spread into a slow nasty smile, revealing jagged black teeth. Even though it was a warm spring day, I felt a coldness envelop my body as my eyes looked straight into his. When the watering can was empty, Beezlebag vanished. I ran inside, soaked and shaking.

'Grandma, Beezlebag just poured something over me.'

'For goodness' sake, child, get in the shower and wash yourself. It's weedkiller. That's the reason I never grow anything at the bottom of the garden. He doesn't want anything coming over onto his side, so he's killed everything I've ever planted there.'

I ran upstairs to wash myself. Grandma was in the kitchen when I came back down.

'Grandma, why doesn't Beezlebag like plants?' I asked.

Beezlebag's garden was devoid of any living thing; it was concreted from back to front like a prison yard.

'When I came here many years ago, a young couple with a baby lived next door. I used to see them with him in his pram. Gorgeous, he was, with a chubby little face and golden hair. Then, all of a sudden, I stopped seeing them out with the baby, just on their own now and again. They seemed to have aged overnight. After about ten years, I stopped seeing them altogether. Apparently, they'd gone, leaving a child on its own in the house.'

I began to tremble. I had heard this story before and I had a terrible feeling I knew what was coming next.

'There were rumours there had been a Spriggan raid and their baby had been taken, leaving a Spriggan baby in his place. I don't know if it's true but I do know that the man next door is a nasty piece of work, and as ugly as the devil.'

Memories came flooding back to me: memories of the boys from Cork and Uncle Ned's story of the changelings.

Grandma's voice seemed to come from far away.

'If you keep away from him and don't bother him, you'll be okay. He doesn't come out of his house much, so you'll hardly ever see him.'

I could feel my legs going weak so I sat down.

'Grandma, what would happen if he managed to get hold of your hair-growing remedy?' I asked, dreading the answer.

'He'd better not. It would be unthinkable. It would start with visits from the men in suits. Then they'd come into the woods searching for the ingredients. I know because when word first spread about it, they spent years harassing me.

'I saw them off, one by one, but if Beezlebag gets hold of my recipe they'll come back, the woods will be devastated and all the occupants will be left homeless. Keep away from him and never ever speak to him. He's bad news.'

I squirmed in my seat, avoiding Grandma's gaze.

I skulked upstairs and looked out of my window. Beezlebag was in his kitchen, taking something out of his fridge.

He took out a large dish of something that looked like raw meat and tipped it down his throat, crimson blood trickling down the sides of his mouth and onto his shirt.

I remembered Uncle Ned telling me that Spriggans only eat raw meat! And I was staring at one, large as life and living right next door. My whole body shivered with fear and goosebumps prickled my skin. I quickly closed the curtains

Chapter
20

The Nightmares Return

The dreamcatcher started to spin wildly.

I stood on the windowsill of my home in Ballybay with the siseesh howling round the house. The window was open and I was listening to the laughter and the children's voices. I didn't know where they were coming from but they were calling my name, coaxing me: Come on, Noola O'Brien. Come play with us. Don't be a scaredy cat. Jump, jump!

I felt the breeze caress my face. It was soft and warm and comforting. I turned round. Uncle Ned was nowhere to be seen. This time, I took a deep breath and … jumped.

I didn't fall to the ground like Uncle Ned had said I would. Instead, I was flying, floating along, surrounded by elves and pixies, witches and goblins. A young pixie took hold of my hand.

'Come on, Noola. Watch me, then do what I do. It's great fun.' The pixie started doing somersaults in the air. I followed. I had never been able to do a handstand or even a cartwheel, but up here, flying through the air, it was easy. I copied the pixie. All I had to do was put my arms out in front of me and kick my legs. My body just went where my arms pointed. It was wonderful. Elves, pixies, witches and goblins were flying past me.

After a few minutes, I recognised where I was. The steep slopes of a wooded valley appeared on either side. Running through the valley bottom was a canal and a river.

As I flew over Pebble Bridge, Grandma's cottage appeared below. I heard a voice behind me calling my name. 'Noola, wait for me. I'm behind you.' I let go of the pixie's hand and looked behind. It was Uncle Ned and he was flying, and from the smile on his face he was enjoying it, too. As he came alongside me, he took my hand.

'Come on, Noola!' he shouted. 'We're nearly there!'

But I couldn't move. Someone or something had hold of my ankle. I looked down to see Beezlebag pulling me towards him. Pebble Bridge had disappeared and I was being dragged down into a black hole. I pulled against Beezlebag with all my strength but it was impossible; he was too strong. I was sinking, down and down.

Beezlebag's pocked face was coming closer until I could smell his foul, stinking breath warm on my face.

'Uncle Ned, help me, help me!' I screamed.

I awoke in bed, my pyjamas soaked with sweat. I sobbed, pushing my face into my pillow so I didn't waken Grandma. The pain in my chest was real, the terror of Beezlebag pulling me down still with me. I looked at the dreamcatcher. At its centre were two bright red glowing eyes staring straight at me. I gripped the covers, pulling them over my head. I could hear a voice in the darkness; it seemed to come from far away, distant and carried by the wind.

'Even when I'm not around, I'll be with you. I'll always be with you.'

They were the same words Uncle Ned had said to me on my birthday. I couldn't still be dreaming - I wasn't asleep.

The wind chime started to tinkle loudly, but it couldn't be the wind, my window was shut. I peeped out from under the covers to see what was happening.

A beam of light from a lone star was shining through the window, lighting up the patchwork squares of the bedspread.

The eyes disappeared and I felt a warmth from my medallion. It radiated through my body as I remembered Uncle Ned's words.

'One day, you'll have to stand on your own two feet and the medallion will help you.'

It warmed me as if I was standing in front of a roaring fire.

I had been holding Uncle Ned's hand, and for a few moments I'd been happy again but now he was gone - on the siseesh. But if it hadn't taken him - well, the alternative was too awful to even contemplate.

Chapter
21

Daddy

After the episode with Beezlebag I avoided the back garden, coming in through the front door. The following day I had to squeeze past a dirty white van parked on the pavement to get through the gate.

The front garden was smaller than the back, but much prettier with a small patch for herbs and flowers in pots. It was Friday and I was looking forward to the weekend.

Buddy shouted before I had chance to hang up my bag.

'Your Grandma's gone out. You've missed all the fun. It's been like World War three in here.' He started to laugh, flicking on the TV.

'She threatened him with the poker.'

'Threatened who with the poker?' I asked, noticing the night cover over Jonjo's cage. 'Why's that over Jonjo so early?'

'You've got a visitor - he's in the back garden,' said Buddy still chuckling.

I froze.

'Who's in the back garden?'

'Your grandma chucked him out; he's waiting to see you.'

I threw down my bag and raced through the kitchen, nearly pulling the door off its hinges.

'Uncle Ned! Uncle Ned!' I shouted. I ran out into the garden to find Daddy leaning on the wall, looking over at the canal.

My stomach sank like a slowly deflating balloon.

He turned around.

'Hawarye, Noola? You look well,' he said, holding his arms out for a hug. I walked towards him, trying not to show my disappointment. He smelled of cigarettes and whiskey and looked like he'd slept in his clothes. He pulled me away and looked at me.

'You don't seem too pleased to see me.'

'Sorry,' I said. 'I am, honestly, but I thought you were Uncle Ned.' Daddy sighed, looking up at the sky and pushed the hair back off his face.

'Come on, make me a cup of tea. I'm parched, what with the long journey and all that.'

I made the tea while Daddy sat at the kitchen table looking out of the window.

'Your grandma's not very pleased with me and your mammy,' he said. 'I thought she was going to kill me just then. I'm glad she's gone out.' He sipped his tea and looked round the room.

'Weird place she's got here. No wonder your mammy turned out like she did. She said to say hello, by the way.'

'You've seen her then?' I asked, putting down my cup.

'I thought you two hated each other.'

'I don't hate her Noola, but we're better off apart. I've been working in London so I looked her up. She's working in a TV shop.' He laughed quietly.

'She thinks she's won the lottery. She won't come back here but she told me to tell you she'll send for you to come and visit when she gets sorted out.'

He smiled, thinking I'd be pleased. I stirred my tea again, putting in too much sugar. I got up and closed the door. I knew Buddy would be listening and I didn't want him to hear what I was going to say as I knew he'd tell Grandma. Sitting down at the table I spoke quietly.

'I won't be going to London to visit Mammy because I'm going to the fair to find Uncle Ned, and then we'll be going home.' I looked up. Daddy's smile had gone and I thought he must be angry because he got up suddenly and rinsed his cup out.

'How long are you staying?' I asked, knowing the answer already. Daddy never hung around for long.

'I'd better be going before your grandma gets back. I want to get out in one piece,' he said, getting himself a drink of water. He turned round and sat down again leaning over the table.

'Noola, about your Uncle Ned.' He took a long drink of water and put the glass down, his face grim and serious.

I waited, taking a sip of my sickly sweet tea.

He opened his mouth to say something when we both heard the front door open. Buddy sounded gleeful.

'He's still here, they're in the kitchen.' Daddy jumped up, ruffling my hair on his way past.

'Bye Noola. I'll come and see you again soon, I promise.'

He opened the door and ran out, escaping through the back gate. Grandma came into the kitchen with a concerned look on her face.

'Are you okay?' She said, shutting the door and putting the kettle on.

'Yes, I'm fine,' I said, going to the sink to throw my tea away. She looked at me and smiled.

'Yes, I think you are,' she said.

Chapter

22

Fred Scratcher

It was two weeks away from the fair, and the weekend had brought the first sunny day of the year. Me and Katy were in Grandma's back garden where Katy was swinging in the hammock, attached to two ragged old apple trees. She was singing along to the radio, her skirt pulled up to reveal her bright white thighs.

She was babbling on about the "Handmade Parade", where every year the people of the community make giant puppets and parade them through the town.

'You know, Katy, your voice is amazing. I really believe one day you will be a singer and actress,' I said.

'I know. I've been chosen as the Pageant Queen in the Parade, because I have such a beautiful voice. I'm in the first float leading the procession. I've got four maids, all the prettiest girls in the year.'

I frowned and carried on potting up some marigolds.

'What are you wearing for the parade?' asked Katy.

'Mummy's having me a dress made. It's Gucci, proper beautiful, cream with sequins and beads and stuff.'

'I'm not in the parade, but I'm not bothered because I hate crowds.' Katy stared at me for a moment before starting to swing the hammock.

'Really, Noola, you're so boring.'

I flushed.

'I think fancy dresses are boring, actually. Nature's much more interesting.' Katy rolled her eyes and laughed. Her voice became shrill and whiny.

'What? You think slugs and snails and stupid plants are better than pretty dresses. Well, I think they're disgusting.'

She lay back down and pulled a ringlet of hair from her fringe, looking at it closely. 'I'm going to the hairdresser's to have my hair done. I'm going with Evie and Iris Grimshaw. They're twins - identical; they're two of my maids in the procession.'

I walked away to the far side of the garden to plant out some seedlings. Katy was beginning to get on my nerves.

I watched a field cuckoo bumblebee settle on a bush next to me and listened to it sing along with Katy to the tune on the radio. Suddenly, Katy let out a high-pitched scream and toppled out of the hammock.

'Did you see that? Some freak was watching us over the fence,' she shrieked. I turned round, but the culprit had gone.

'Do something, Noola! Call the police!' wailed Katy, who was hysterical by now.

'That was Beezlebag, the man next door. He's creepy, but he won't harm you, and the police won't do anything. They're scared of him,' I said.

'Well, tell your grandma to turn him into a slug or something. She is a witch, after all.'

'She can't,' I replied. 'The last time he did something bad she tried to turn him into a chicken, but he just grew feathers out of his head. Transfiguration isn't her strong point.'

'Oh, why did Mummy bring me to this town? It's full of weirdos and freaks, and you and your grandma, you're fraudsters. I'm going to Evie and Iris's house.'

She stamped off, slamming the gate behind her. I was stunned. As far as I'd seen, Beezlebag had just been gawping at us over the fence. From katy's reaction you'd think he'd tied us up and kidnapped us. She really would make a great actress.

Tears trickled down my face. Katy might never talk to me again and it was all Beezlebag's fault. I couldn't understand why Katy had been so mean. If this is what having friends was like, maybe Id be better off on my own. I lay back in the hammock and thought of home in Ballybay. The beach, surrounded by the steep limestone cliffs, the stillness of the sea on a sunny day and the feeling that it goes on forever, the wildness of the crashing waves after a storm…and Uncle Ned. I looked up at the sky and watched the great banks of fluffy clouds hurrying by. The hillside rose steeply on either side of me like the shoulders of giants shielding this strange town from prying eyes.

'I hate it here. Where are you, Uncle Ned? I want to go home,' I whispered.

I lay in the hammock thinking things over. It was only two weeks until the fair and I still hadn't done any transfiguration. I dried my eyes and pulled myself out; now was as good a time as any. I found the place where I'd planted the gurglegit seedlings. It was incredible. A week ago, the plants were five centimetres high, now they were fifty centimetres. Dangling from their stalks were huge pods. I pulled one off and popped it open. Inside were eight big pink seeds. Putting them in my pocket, I ran upstairs to get the necklace from Juli Anabaluloo. It was time to put it to the test.

I headed for the canal where colourful narrowboats were tied up along the towpath. Walking along, I could hear voices coming from one of the boats.

'Fred, wash those dishes for me, will you?'

I noticed Fred Scratcher sitting on top of the boat.

'Where ye goin?' he asked. 'Can I come?' He jumped off the narrowboat and started to walk alongside me. I gave him a sideways glance and ignored him.

'I'm sorry about Gobbit. I don't like him but I put up with him coz I've never had any mates,' said Fred.

'Live on a narrowboat, see, so I've never been in one place long enough to make friends. He's the first mate I've ever had. If you're not friends with him no one talks to you. That's why no one talks to you - they're scared to.'

'Well, I'd rather be on my own forever than be friends with an ape like him,' I said.

I looked at Fred, who stared down at his feet as two rosy spots appeared on his cheeks. I studied him closely. He had a nice face, too nice for a boy, with long eyelashes and the bluest of eyes. A strange sensation fluttered in my tummy as if it were full of butterflies. I understood why he wanted a friend so much, why he didn't want to be on his own.

'What's it like living with a witch?' he asked.

'It's great. My Grandma's a good witch, she helps people,' I said, 'and I'm going to be a witch, too.'

We had walked for about ten minutes and were approaching a rather overgrown part of the canal.

'Goose juice, that's the answer.'

I looked at Fred. 'What did you say?'

'Din't say nuffin. It was that duck over there squawking.'

As we rounded the corner, a large black and white duck with a red face was rolling about on the ground covering itself in goose poo.

'What are you doing that for?' I asked the duck.

'Camouflage. I'm a private detective. Ivan the Muscovy at your service,' replied the duck.

'But why cover yourself in poo?' I asked. I wanted to hold my nose but thought it might seem impolite. The poo smelled disgusting.

'I'm going undercover. My white feathers give me away so I need it for camouflage.'

'Oh, I see,' I said.

Fred stood staring at me. All he could hear was me talking to the duck and the duck quacking.

'I'm Noola, and this is Fred Scratcher. He lives on a boat.'

'Pleased to meet you,' said Ivan.

'Why are you going undercover?' I asked.

'Special assignment, top secret,' said Ivan. 'Must go, time is ticking. If you ever need a detective, just ask any of the birds. They'll send out a hoot and I'll come to your assistance.'

Ivan plopped into the canal, swam to the other side and waddled off into the woods opposite. Fred stared at me.

'You were talking to that duck like it could understand you. Blimey, Gobbit was right. He said he'd seen you talking to the pigeons on the bike shed at school. Can you understand them, can you really?'

Just at that moment, Fred's mum came past in the narrowboat. She shouted to him.

'Hey, you, what d'ya think you're doing sneaking off like that?' She didn't look annoyed - she was smiling.

She looks more like his sister than his mum, I thought. She had short blonde hair and masses of freckles. Her eyes were vivid blue, the same blue as the pansies in Grandma's garden. The same blue as Fred's.

'D'ya want to come for a ride?' asked Fred. 'I want to show you something.' Fred's mum steered the boat into the side for him to get on. He reached out a hand to me.

Yes, why not? I thought. I'd never been on a narrowboat. I took his hand and jumped on board.

'Mum, this is Noola. Her grandma is Isabel, you know, the witch.'

'Hi, Noola. Pleased to meet you. Fred's told me all about you. I think he's quite fascinated by you.' Fred's mum smiled.

I felt myself blushing.

'Hi, Mrs Scratcher. I like your boat,' I said.

I followed Fred down two small steps into the galley below and then down a short corridor which led to his room.

In the room was a bed and a wardrobe with just enough room to walk in between. Fred pulled out a box from under the bed. Inside it was a baby bird. He gently took it out.

'I think it's got a broken wing.'

I looked down at the pitiful creature.

'I can't mend its wing, but maybe I can help it fly again.'

I took out my mobile phone.

'Here, Fred, video this,' I said, passing it to him. He took the phone, slightly puzzled and started recording. I took the seeds out of my pocket and broke them into tiny pieces. The bird nibbled them and pecked at my hand for more. I took out the necklace, aware of Fred watching me intently.

Excited now, I started to rub the necklace.

'Mumbago Tibiago Malawi Dijango,' I chanted.

Nothing happened.

I placed my hand on the bird and chanted again.

'Mumbago Tibiago Malawi Dijango.' This time, a rush of heat seared up my arm and the bird started to grow. As I chanted faster and faster, a mist surrounded me, and a flash of blue lit up the room. Fred dived under the bed and I felt my body being flung back towards the door.

When the mist cleared, I rubbed my eyes. There, sitting in the middle of the bed, was a huge Canada goose.

Fred crawled out from under the bed and stared at it. 'Whoa,' he said, throwing my phone at me and disappearing out of the room. I sat on the bed in shock and stared at the goose. I finished the video and after a few minutes, Fred peeped round the door. A huge grin spread across his face. 'Wow! That was amazing - you're amazing,' he said, grinning broadly. I could feel myself going crimson again so I fumbled with my phone, willing my face to cool down.

Fred stroked the bird.

'I think we'd better let it go,' he said.

'It's the first time I've done that,' I said.

'I meant to change it into a pigeon. I think I need more practice. Never mind, at least its wing's not broken any more. Come on, we'll put it in the canal.'

We carried the huge goose upstairs between us and put it into the water, where it swam off to join the other geese.

'I need to go home now. Grandma will be worried about me,' I said.

'Thanks Noola I've had the best afternoon ever,' said Fred, helping me off the boat. I blushed for the third time in half an hour.

Chapter

23

Top of the Class

I watched from a distance as Katy walked arm in arm between Iris and Evie Grimshaw. I looked up at the miserable watery grey sky which perfectly matched my mood and thought about what Grandma had said. Why did grown-ups always have to be right. A familiar feeing of sadness washed over me and I longed to be back home with Uncle Ned.

I opened my book but couldn't concentrate. I could hear Katy laughing now. I looked up to see Fred running through the playground gates, bounding towards me like an over-excited puppy.

'Hi, Noola,' he said, jumping onto the wall next to me. 'I've got something to show you.' He reached into his bag and pulled out a sketchpad. I took the pad and opened it. Inside were sketches of the wildlife along the canal.

'Did you do these?' I asked. Fred nodded.

'They're brilliant,' I said. 'You could sell these.'

'D'ya think so?'

I nodded as I flicked through the pages.

'I wish I could, My mum could do with the money.'

'I bet she's really proud of you,' I said.

'She hasn't seen most of them. I do them when she's asleep. She's been a bit poorly recently, that's why we've stayed in Pebble Bridge so long. Normally, we would've moved on by now.'

'I'd buy one,' I said, looking at Fred. He smiled, his face flushed with pleasure. It occurred to me that I had much more in common with Fred than Katy.

The last sketch was of a heron catching a fish. It looked practically lifelike.

'Amazing,' I said, turning to Fred and handing him the book.

'Not as cool as you turning that baby bird into a goose. That's what I call amazing,' said Fred. I sighed.

'But it didn't work. I meant to change it into a pigeon. I need more practice but I don't know who to practise on.'

'There's loads of ducks on the canal; practise on one of them.'

'I can't go round picking on any old duck. What if it likes being a duck?'

'Well, yes, I suppose you're right. I never thought of that.'

The bell rang and we jumped off the wall and headed into school.

'Thanks, Fred. You've just given me an idea. That Muscovy duck had to roll round in goose poo for camouflage. I bet he wouldn't mind being changed into something else. I'll go find him after school and ask him.'

The day dragged as I sat looking out of the window. A knot of anxiety had lodged in my stomach. If I couldn't master transfiguration, it was game over. I'd never be able to go to the fair and find Uncle Ned.

In the afternoon, Miss Newt made an announcement

'Today, we're going to assess your school projects. Now, I did ask you all to write a statement about how to improve our environment, but it seems most of you didn't seem to grasp the concept. Rodney seems to think the answer is to annihilate all the squirrels in Pebble Bridge.' A wave of laughter rippled round the class. Miss Newt continued.

'And Katy seems to think the answer is to open a nail bar.'

Katy scowled as the laughter grew louder.

'Be quiet, everyone,' shouted Miss Newt.

'Fred, you didn't write enough but your art work is exceptional. You're a very talented artist but I needed a statement as well. And, Ethan, your idea about bat boxes was pretty good but you didn't do your research as I asked you to. Bats don't live in bird nesting boxes.'

'But miss, bats are an endangered species. All their usual nesting places are disappearing,' he answered.

'Yes, Ethan, but council funds won't stretch to putting bat boxes on every house in Pebble Bridge.' Miss Newt cast a beaming smile in my direction. I turned round to see who she could possibly be smiling at.

'Only Noola O'Brien came up with anything worth listening to. Well done Noola.' I flushed, wishing the idea had been mine.

'I'd like you to come up here and read it out.'

My legs felt wobbly as I walked to the front of the class. As I faced them their faces swam in front of me. Rodney scowled and Katy watched sulkily as I took the project from Miss Newt. I tried to speak but the words caught in my throat and came out as a small croak. The class erupted into fresh giggles.

'That's enough,' ordered Miss Newt sternly.

I shut my eyes tightly and pictured Buddy. I felt the warmth from the St Christopher round my neck and as I opened them, Fred caught my eye and smiled. That was all the help I needed. I began to read.

"At first they called it global warming. Then it became climate change. Now it's a climate crisis.

Apparently, the scientists have been banging on about it for thirty years.'

I paused for dramatic effect and raised my voice.

'I SAY, THEY DIDN'T SHOUT LOUD ENOUGH.

Apparently, the scientists are going to start making great Carbon-guzzling machines to trap the carbon and stop global warming. BUT IT'S TOO LATE. And besides, don't they know that the most efficient carbon-guzzling machines in the world have been around for millions of years: THEY'RE CALLED TREES So, I say, to improve the environment we need to change the way we live, plant more trees and stop chopping them down."

Miss Newt stood up and started to clap, her black cloak billowing behind her. Fred stood up and joined in and one after another, all the class joined in too. I noticed that Rodney and Katy were the only ones still sitting.

'Well done Noola, for your excellent effort, you will be getting the award for the most improved student this term and as a special treat I would like you to be the Green Man in our Save our Planet float at the Handmade Parade on Saturday.' I swallowed hard before saying,

'Thank you, Miss Newt.'

This was a disaster. Saturday was the day I was going to the fair to find Uncle Ned. The Handmade Parade didn't finish until one. Dill had told me they were setting off at one. I'd have to stall them somehow.

A feeling of panic gripped me. I still needed to master transfiguration and pass my theory exam - and I had only three days to do it.

Chapter
24

Ivan the Squirrel

After school, I found Syd and Charlie in their usual spot on top of the bike shed.

'Would you put a hoot out for Ivan the Muscovy and ask him to meet me at Dill Cobnutt's house?' I asked.

'Aye lass,' said Syd. 'No bother, he'll be on the canal somewhere. What time shall I say?'

'About six o'clock, thanks,' I said, hurrying away.

'Well done, Noola,' said Buddy, reading my certificate. 'Put it on the mantelpiece.' Grandma was cleaning out Jonjo's cage while he paced up and down behind her.

'My prize is to be the Green Man in the Save our Planet Float on Saturday. I have to dress in a costume made from leaves, as apparently, the green man is a nature spirit, a symbol of the ancient forests that once covered the lands'

I said through a mouthful of beans on toast.

'That's fantastic,' roared Buddy, sending Jonjo scuttling up Grandma's back, over her head and back into his cage.

Grandma gave up in disgust. She stood up, pushing her glasses from the tip of her nose and looked at the certificate. Settling down in one of the large armchairs, she studied me intently.

'Yes, well done, Noola. You know you never cease to amaze me.'

Jonjo circled his cage watching Buddy fearfully. Grandma scowled,

'Did you have to shout so loud Buddy, you've frightened Jonjo again.'

'But it's brilliant. The parade is the perfect platform for the launch of my tree planting campaign. I'll order a banner off the Internet and Noola can attach it to the float,' said Buddy.

'I don't know about that,' I said, wishing I hadn't told him.

'But Noola, the publicity will be amazing; it's just what I need,' said Buddy.

'Okay,' I said, 'seeing as it was your statement that won the prize, but don't make it too big. I'm not sure if Miss Newt will approve.' Silently, I didn't care. Hopefully, if all went to plan, I'd be going home anyway and never going back to school.

'I'm going out for a bit, Grandma,' I said, picking up my last piece of toast. 'I won't be long. I'll do the dishes when I get back.'

I walked across the bridge and climbed the steps to the woods.

As I neared the clearing in front of Sorrel's house, a young deer with Dillon riding on its back came hurtling towards me. I jumped out of the way as the deer galloped past, bucking Dill off and catapulting him into a ditch. I ran over and pulled him out.

'Catch yourself on, Dillon Cobnutt. One of these days you're going to get yourself killed.' Dill grinned.

'Ah yes, but I'll have fun doing it.'

As we were speaking, Ivan the Muscovy hurtled out of the sky like a small out-of-control plane landing with a bump in the clearing. He was a huge duck and not accustomed to flying. In fact, he only took to the sky in extreme emergencies. He composed himself and waddled over to us.

'What's to do, pixie? Half the birds in the valley have been putting out hoots for me. What's happened?'

'Nothing's happened,' I replied, 'but I've been thinking, I might be able to help you.' Ivan started to waddle up and down.

'What on earth are you talking about? Look, I'm a very busy goose I haven't time to stand here gossiping.'

'How would you feel about being something else?'

'What do you mean, like what?'

'How would you feel about being a squirrel?' I asked.

'Mmm, never thought about it before,' said Ivan, scratching his feathers with his beak.

'I suppose it would make me a little less conspicuous.'

I took the fruit from the Gurglegit plant out of my pocket as Dill watched, his eyes as big as golf balls. I snapped it open to reveal the bright pink seeds.

'Here, eat these,' I said. Ivan ate the seeds and looked up at me. 'Well, that didn't work, did it?'

I took the necklace out of my pocket. Dill shot towards me.

'Wow, a voodoo amulet. Where did you get that from? Do you know how to use it?' he asked, jumping up and down as if he had springs attached to his feet.

'A friend gave it to me and I sort of know how to use it; it kind of worked last time. Here, take my phone and video it for me,' I said, passing Dill the phone. I started to rub the necklace.

'Mumbago Tibiago Malawi Dijango' I chanted. I stared at Ivan and imagined him as a squirrel. Nothing happened.

I placed my hand on his back and chanted again. This time he began to shrink - feathers started to fly. I chanted faster and faster, rubbing the necklace furiously. A surge of heat shot up my arm. A flash of crimson smoke exploded from it, and with a huge bang, as if someone had set off a firecracker, I was thrown back onto the grass. The smoke cleared and a small red squirrel appeared in front of us.

Dill dropped my phone and snatched the amulet out of my hands. Red fur started to cover his fingers and hands and creep up his arms.

'Aaargh, aaargh!' He screamed, throwing the necklace onto the grass. I picked up the phone and finished the video before looking at Dill. He looked like he was turning into a rabbit.

'Oh, for goodness' sake, what did you have to go and do that for?' I said.

'Do something, Noola. I can't go round looking like a rodent,' he said, tugging at his furry arms.

'Don't worry, I'll get you some of Grandma's hair-removing lotion.'

Ivan, delirious, bounced up and down in front of us.

'Wow, that was amazing,' he said, doing a backflip and bouncing off the nearest tree. 'I'm never gonna be a clumsy duck again.'

'Well, I'm really glad you feel that way because I don't know how to change you back,' I said, picking up the necklace and walking away, leaving Dill still tugging at his arms while Ivan scampered off into the woods.

As I walked home, my mind was reeling. I'd done it! Now all I needed to do was pass my theory test, but time was running out. I was setting off for the fair in three days. I couldn't put it off any longer.

I should have been excited but the thought of going to the fair now filled me with dread. What if Uncle Ned wasn't there? Life had been so simple in Ballybay, here it was so complicated. Katy, who I thought was my friend, had turned out to be shallow, and Fred who I thought was horrible, had turned out to be nice, really nice.

I arrived home, ran inside and up to my room. I logged on to the website "world of witches" and brought up the theory questions. They were multiple choice and the first one was, "List the ingredients for an affecting potion" I exhaled slowly - this might be easier than I'd imagined.

I finished the exam in less than an hour and signed Grandma's signature electronically. I added the transfiguration video as an attachment and clicked the send button, full of confidence. I had read every book in Grandma's cellar twice over. I should get the results tomorrow.

Chapter

25

The Man from the Pharmaceuticals

The following morning, I woke up to the sound of hammering next door. I looked out of the window to see Beezlebag and another elf lifting a large wooden crate onto a rusty old pickup. The pickup was loaded with at least five more crates. The elf was nearly as ugly as Beezlebag. One side of his face was disfigured with a hideous bright red scar which stretched from his forehead to his chin.

As they worked, a blue estate car pulled up and a smart-looking man with a briefcase got out. The man looked official, and he was wearing a suit! I started to shake uncontrollably.

He must be from the pharmaceuticals…he'd come for the hair-growing remedy.

Pulling on my clothes, I ran downstairs and out of the door to the bottom of the garden and peeped through a hole in the fence.

'Is this it?' said the man in the suit.

'Well, that's the recipe, Mr Beardsworth,' said Beezlebag.

The man scanned the sheet of paper and looked at Beezlebag with contempt.

'You might as well have given me a list saying doggy doo and cat poo as this list. I need a sample, something to test,' he replied.

'Well, you see the ingredients are quite strange,' said Beezlebag, scratching his chin.

'I can tell you where to get them though.'

'Come back to me when you have a sample, and stop wasting my time,' replied the man, his voice receding into the distance as he spoke. I heard a car door slam.

'Well, that didn't go to plan did it. I thought you said they'd be falling over themselves to get your magic recipe,' said Beezlebag's companion.

'You wait, they will. I just need to make a sample. She gets the ingredients from the woods. 'We'll go on Saturday when we've finished the other business.'

'Ye nicked the last lot of ingredients from 'er 'ouse, din't ye?'

'Yes, but I might not be able to get in 'er house again. I can get most of the ingredients off the Internet, apart from the fairies' wings and the twerts, and they can't be that hard to find.'

'But she knows how to find 'em; she's got a degree in witchcraft.'

'Oh shut up Scarface and help me with this crate.'

I jumped up and ran inside. I'd suddenly remembered my exam results would be through this morning. I ran up to my bedroom and switched on my computer which seemed to take forever to warm up.

Logging on to my emails, I saw the words:

Congratulations, you have successfully completed the online theory and potion requirement for your witch's apprenticeship certification. (GRADE 1)

Please click on the link below to print your certificate.

I'd done it! I flopped backwards onto my bed and punched the air. I started to laugh and cry at the same time, picking up the photo of Uncle Ned and hugging it to my chest. There was no time to lose now. I jumped up and turned on my printer and printed off the certificate, then logged onto the witches' web to get my ticket to the fair. As I listened to the rhythmic phut-phut of the printer I glanced out of the window where Beezlebag and his mate were lifting the last of the crates onto the pickup. My good mood disappeared in an instant. What were the crates for- and what was the other business he was planning? It seemed that no sooner had I overcome one problem, I had another one to add to my growing list.

Chapter
26

The Handmade Parade

I stood behind the kitchen door, listening. Grandma was cooking and had the phone on loudspeaker. She came straight out with it.

'Lula, I think the reason Nigel Dunderfield wants to go out with you is because Noola gave him a love philtre and it worked.'

'Don't be ridiculous. How could she?'

A bead of sweat trickled down my face as I tried to quiet my breathing. I had been found out!

For a moment, the line went quiet until Lula carried on.

'Hang on, she was fidgeting with something when I took her to the doctors, now I come to think of it.'

Lula's voice became high pitched and angry.

'I wouldn't go out with that man if he was the only man in Pebble Bridge. The pompous arrogant twit.'

'I told you that weeks ago,' said Grandma, 'and I told you he'd never go out with you.'

'Yes, and Noola was there when you said it. That's why she did it. When you think about it Isabel, it was a very kind gesture.' Grandma was quiet for a moment before she spoke.

'You know, she's not as docile as I first thought, because it's not the only thing. Rodney Gobbit's remedy, I think she might have had something to do with that not working as well - she must have. I made the remedy as I've always done.

It's too much of a coincidence. I've suspected she's been up to something for a while.'

My face became hot. Grandma knew everything. She was sure to ring the social workers now. It's a good job I was going to the fair to find Uncle Ned otherwise I'd be destined for the children's home for sure.

I wanted to run away but I carried on listening

'Is Noola okay Isabel? She seemed a little bit quiet the last time I saw her,' said Lula.

'Her friend Katy's fallen out with her. I don't know why, over something and nothing I expect.'

'You're lucky to have Noola you know, and as for that Clapshot girl, she's not Noola's type. Maybe it's a good thing they've fallen out,' said Lula.

'Well, I know one thing, the house has never been so clean and she makes the most delicious soda bread.'

'I wish I had a granddaughter like her. She'd make a great apprentice, you know. Anyway, I'll have to go. I'm opening the shop early today. It's the Handmade Parade. Should be busy. Town's heaving already.'

'I'm going to the woods, out of the way. I can't stand the crowds. Are you sure you don't mind looking after Noola for a few days while I'm away at the fair? I'm setting off with Dill at one o'clock.'

'Not at all,' replied Lula. 'I'm looking forward to the company. Tell her to call at the shop with her things. I'll speak to you when you get back.'

I went upstairs to get ready for the Handmade Parade. All the children of the valley had been going to weekend workshops for months to help make the giant puppets. There would be a party atmosphere in town but I wasn't in the mood for a party.

I put on the Green Man suit Miss Newt had given me. The body, shaped like a cone, was covered in green paper

leaves with holes for my arms. To go with it, I had to wear
fluorescent green tights and a mask made of leaves cut out
of felt. 'I look like a Christmas tree with a mouldy lettuce on
top,' I thought as I looked in the mirror. I paced up and down
my bedroom, biting my nails. I had waited so long for this
day but now it was here, I wasn't ready.

'Noola, hurry up. You're going to be late,' shouted
Grandma from the bottom of the stairs.

She was acting as if nothing had happened. She'd most
likely be getting the foster home set up before she confronted
me with the evidence.

I took out a small package from my top drawer and read
the label, VALERIAN ROOT. MAKES THE RECIPIENT
DROWSY AND UNSTEADY ON THEIR FEET. I had
ordered it off the internet earlier in the week. I went into the
kitchen to make Grandma some tea, adding a teaspoon of the
ground root and an extra teaspoon of sugar to disguise the
taste. I packed my bag and set off into town, unable to shake
off the guilty feeling that had been with me all morning. I'd

done a terrible thing drugging Grandma but if I couldn't get to the fair, I'd never find Uncle Ned.

I entered the Town Hall where everyone was waiting for the parade to start. Spotting Katy, I headed towards her.

She stood in her sequinned and beaded dress, surrounded by Evie and Iris Grimshaw and two other girls who all looked like bridesmaids at her wedding.

'Hi Katy,' I said.

Katy looked at me dressed in my Greenman suit and sniggered. 'Some people just don't get the message,' she said, walking off arm in arm with Evie Grimshaw.

I looked down at my green legs as heat flooded my face. I felt a sudden urge to run home and hide, until I spotted Miss Newt in the distance waving over at me like my new best friend. I clambered aboard the float with Rodney, Roland and two other boys dressed as trees who all stood at the front, well away from me, and took out Buddy's banner.

'Here Gobbit, hold this,' I said, handing him one end.

'Get lost,' said Rodney. 'Just coz you're suddenly teachers pet doesn't mean you can start bossing me about.'

'Tie it to the float,' I said sharply, 'if you don't want you and your family to end up as hairy as a bunch of badgers.'

Rodney grudgingly picked up one end of the banner.

'Ere Roland, grab 'old o' the other end.' The banner flapped in the breeze until Rodney secured it to the front of the float.

I jumped off the float and snapped a picture to show to Buddy.

YOUR PLANET NEEDS YOU! JOIN BUDDY'S ARMY-PLANT SOME TREES. Join us at www.Buddy's.army.co.uk.

The town heaved with crowds of tourists and locals as the samba band started up and the parade headed into the main street. I ducked down behind a bale of hay and watched the

float behind. It was full of elves dressed in colourful green, scarlet and gold costumes. I couldn't recall seeing any of them before. They jumped on and off the float, handing out dolls to babies and toddlers in pushchairs. I spotted one of them giving a doll to Katy's little sister, Erin Rose. She was only eighteen months old and didn't have Katy's buck teeth. Her blonde hair fell in ringlets round her rosy cheeks. She was beautiful. She laughed as she grabbed the doll and hugged it.

It was nearing the end of the parade. As the floats were heading over the bridge to the park, I realised what was happening. I saw another elf jump off the float behind and hand out a doll to another lovely little blonde girl. There was something familiar about him, so I leaned forward for a closer look. It was Beezlebag!

I started to tremble as Uncle Ned's words came back to me:

Spriggans are dangerous. They only take fair-haired babies and only the most beautiful ones. They dress in vivid green scarlet and gold. They are villains, thieves, gangsters.

An icy cold chill crept up my spine.

THE CRATES!

The elves were dressed in the same green scarlet and gold and amongst them was Beezlebag! I watched, unable to take my eyes off him.

There must be something in the dolls. I had to get hold of one to find out what it was. If it was what I thought it would be, the children of the town were in very big trouble.

The floats stopped in the park where the samba band started up again. I jumped off the float and threaded my way through jugglers, stilt men and clowns, looking for Katy's mum and sister. I eventually found her and her boyfriend watching a fire-eater.

'Hi, Mrs Clapshot. Shall I take Erin for an ice cream?' I asked. Katy's mum was nothing like my own mother. She was dressed in tight jeans and high-heeled shoes. Her short blonde hair was cut into a fashionable bob and she was engrossed in conversation with her latest boyfriend, the one she'd met on the internet dating site, the one she'd uprooted her family and travelled hundreds of miles for.

'Oh yeah, Noola, she'd love that,' answered Katy's mum.

I bought Erin an ice cream and took her into the shrubbery which circled the park. I gave her the ice cream in exchange for the doll. The doll was a miniature replica of the Spriggans. It was made from cloth and dressed in green breeches, a gold waistcoat and a scarlet jacket. Its pointed hat finished off with a feather was the same green as its breeches. I removed its clothes carefully and ripped a hole in its back. Inside was a GPS receiver.

Images of the changelings flashed through my mind and a wave of sickness washed over me. Why did this have to happen today of all days?

Erin had now finished the ice cream and was screaming for the doll back. I quickly dressed the doll and gave it to her before someone came to see what was happening.

I took Erin back to her mother and set off home, looking at my watch. The time said ten to one. I started to run.

I had to tell Grandma that the Spriggans were going to steal the town's babies and we had to stop them. A feeling of panic gripped me. Maybe Grandma would be asleep, drugged by the valerian root.

As I left the park I nearly tripped over Syd and Charlie, who were busy finishing off the remains of someone's picnic.

'Eee, lass, tha's in a dither. Wot's 'appened?' asked Syd.

'Oh, Syd, am I pleased to see you. Would you send a hoot out for Ivan the Muscovy, I mean, Ivan the Squirrel, and tell him to meet me at Dill Cobnutt's house?'

'Ay lass. Okay, will do,' replied Syd. 'But whatever's the matter?'

'I have to hurry. Just tell Ivan. I'll tell you later.' Syd and Charlie flew off towards the woods as I hurried on.

A little further on I saw Fred and his mum sitting at the side of the canal. He had set up a table outside his narrowboat with framed prints of his wildlife sketches. A group of tourists crowded around them. He spotted me and jumped up.

'Hey, Noola, where are you going in such a hurry?'

I stopped to catch my breath.

'Fred, will you go and find Katy? Tell her that she mustn't let Erin out of her sight.' I was just about to explain about the Spriggans and how Erin had been chosen as one of the children to be swapped, when I realised that Katy wouldn't have a clue about Spriggans and how dangerous they were. It did seem rather far-fetched.

'What's happened?' asked Fred.

'It's the Spriggans. I don't know if you know anything about them, but they're very dangerous. They're in town. They were at the parade giving out dolls to babies and toddlers.'

'What?' said Fred, looking stunned. 'I've heard about the Spriggans. They're evil. They steal human children and swap them, don't they?'

'Yes, the dolls had GPS receivers in them to track the children, and one of the children they gave a doll to was Katy's little sister, Erin.'

'What are you going to do?'

'I'm going to the woods to stop them. Will you warn Katy for me?'

'Yes, okay,' said Fred turning towards the park, 'I'll spread the word so everyone knows. Good luck.'

I started to run, my mind in turmoil. I could pretend it wasn't happening. Katy had been mean and it served her right. It might stop me getting to the fair. I pictured Erin's innocent face and shook my head, shaking the thoughts away.

I arrived home to find Grandma sitting with her foot up on a stool and Doctor Dunderfield pacing up and down on the phone to somebody.

'Whats happened Grandma?' I asked, rushing towards her.

'I've only gone and tripped going up the steps to the woods. I've been feeling strange all day. I managed to limp home but now I'm in agony. Nigel says I've broken my leg and I need to go to hospital.'

I felt a churning in the pit of my stomach. This wasn't meant to happen; this was awful. I'd only meant to make Grandma feel drowsy. 'Are you going to be okay Grandma?' I said, thankful at least that she was awake and could tell me what to do. She winced with pain.

'I hope so, but I'm not going to be able to go to the fair.'

The doctor went into the kitchen to ring the ambulance while I told Grandma about the Spriggans.

'Oh, this is all I need. You'll have to warn the parents,' she said.

'No, Grandma, I don't know who to warn and even if I did, they probably wouldn't believe me. Apart from all that, there isn't time. I can't let them take Erin. Katy would never forgive me.'

The colour drained from her face and for a moment she looked like she was going to faint.

'The pain in my leg is excruciating; there's no way I'm going to be able to go anywhere.' She sighed, a look of resignation on her face.

'Find Dill, he'll sort it. But first, go downstairs. You'll find a potion called "Midge Biting Lotion". It's on the top shelf with the bottles with skull and crossbones and red labels.'

I ran downstairs to the cellar scouring the bottles of the finished potions and reading the labels:

DEADLY NIGHTSHADE, CYANIDE, TOXIC BAT SPIT. There it was, MIDGE BITE EXTRA STRONG BITING FORMULA.

I picked up the bottle, along with a bottle of hair-removing lotion and ran back upstairs.

'Give the Midge biting potion to Dill,' said Grandma. 'Tell him to put it in the Spriggans' cooking pot.

'Now go, before it's too late. As soon as you've given it to him, come back, pack some things and go stay with Lula. Explain what's happened and tell her I'm not going to the fair, Dill will have to go on his own. I should only be in hospital for a day or so.'

I ran upstairs to change out of my Green Man costume and collect my ticket to the fair.

After the ambulance left, I pulled on my boots, put my certificate and ticket in my bag and wrote a note for Grandma. 'Going to the fair with Dill to help him get the shopping.' I stood it on the mantelpiece next to the clock. I sent a text to Lula and told her I wouldn't be coming.

As I crossed the bridge, I heard a loud gurgling croak, throaty and hoarse. I looked up to see Zach circling above.

'Kraa-kraa,' he called, leading me forward, his call urgent and shrill.

'Kraa-kraa,' he called again, heading in the direction of the woods. I started to run, watching Zach until he disappeared into the canopy of leaves.

'That's it, I've got it, now it makes sense,' I murmured. 'Call me when you need me and I'll find them for you.'

Now I knew what to do.

Chapter

27

The Evil Spriggans

Noola, you're here at last, thank goodness,' said Dill. 'Izzy rang and told us what happened at the parade so Poppa's gone to look for Ivan. Come in while he gets here.'

I sat down to catch my breath.

'Talking of Ivan, this is for your furry arms,' I said, taking the hair-removing potion out of my bag and passing it to him. He grabbed the bottle and drank it down in one gulp and I watched in amazement as the fur immediately started to disappear.

The sound of Zach's urgent call from somewhere deep in the woods jolted me back to reality.

'Listen, Dill. You need to send Zach to find where the Spriggans are. We can't waste time looking for them. We haven't got long. They'll be taking the children tonight.'

He jumped up.

'Brilliant, good thinking. I'll go find him,' he said, nearly knocking me over on his way out. I began to pace up and down, the knot of anxiety in my stomach twisting even tighter. In the corner of the room, I spotted a large cage filled with a dead tree trunk covered in ferns. Peeping out from underneath one of them I saw a tiny face with what looked like an upturned buttercup on its head. The face belonged to a tiny flower fairy. It crawled out from behind the fern and ventured towards me. Her arms were folded and she had a defiant expression on her face.

Another fern rustled and another flower fairy appeared, this time with an upturned bluebell on her head.

As I watched them Dill burst through the door.

'Oh, you've found my flitterlings,' he said. 'Cute, aren't they? They're flower fairies. I'm using them as models for my new range of wood carvings; they should do a bomb in Lula's shop.' I looked at the cross little faces.

'Yes, they're beautiful, but I don't think you should have put them in a cage.'

'Oh, it won't be for long. I'll let them go as soon as I've finished with them. Flitterlings are pussycats; they wouldn't harm anyone. I wouldn't catch a tree fairy, though. Those beechlings can be dangerous.'

As we were talking, Sorrel came in. He looked different, younger somehow. His brown wrinkled face didn't seem so wrinkled.

'What's happened to you?' I asked. 'You look different – younger.'

Sorrel smiled. 'Crocodile teeth,' he said. 'But I'll tell you about that later. Ivan's on his way. He'll be here any minute. I need to go pack Dill some sandwiches.'

Dill ran to the window and squinted through.

'Where is he? We should have set off ages ago.'

As he spoke there was a tremendous racket outside as Ivan hurtled out of a tree landing on two stony twerts. They each grabbed one of his legs and started to pull in opposite directions. 'Rip 'is gizzards out,' screamed one of the twerts, as they tried to tear him in two. Howling with pain, Ivan tried to bite the fingers of one of the stony twerts but couldn't reach them.

I shot out of the door after Dill, tripping over a tree root and grabbing him round the waist. The pair of us landed on top of Ivan and the twerts, causing them to let go of him. I jumped out of the way as Dill started to whack the twerts with a big stick and Ivan tumbled back onto the grass wheezing and winded. Ivan fought to catch his breath.

'I need to get the wood warden to sort these blummin' hooligans out. The woods are seething with the horrible things. Anyhow, what's to do, Pixie? What's happened?'

'It's not what's happened but what's going to happen. We need your help. The Spriggans were at the parade giving dolls out to babies. The dolls had GPS receivers in them - they're going to steal the town's babies, and we need to stop them before it's too late.'

'Hang on a minute, go a little slower. Did you say Spriggans?'

'Yes, Spriggan elves. They're going to steal the town's babies and we haven't got time to stand here discussing it. We need to stop them.'

'Okay, okay,' he laughed nervously.' It's a good job I'm not a goose anymore; if those Spriggans get hold of me it would be roast goose for supper. They're an evil bunch. Where are they and what d'ya want me to do?'

I showed Ivan the midge bite potion. 'I want you to put this in their cooking pot.' Zach came back and landed on Dill's shoulder, putting his beak to Dill's ear.

'He's found them, I'll just get my bag and we'll get going. They're about a kilometre this way,' said Dill, pointing into the woods.

We set off. Ivan, delighting in his new identity, scrambled up and down trees, showing off his agility by jumping from one branch to another. After half an hour, we saw smoke in the distance.

'It's the Spriggans' camp,' whispered Dill. 'Get behind me.'

My knees started to buckle. Dill grabbed me to stop me from falling and dragged me behind a huge oak tree while

Ivan climbed to the top. The Spriggans were sitting around a campfire. In cages behind them were the baby Spriggans. They were the same cages Beezlebag had been loading onto the pickup. Each cage had a label with a name and address.

Dill got out his binoculars for a closer look. I grabbed them from him and scanned the labels until I found the one that said, SWAP FOR ERIN ROSE CLAPSHOT.

I gasped. The child in the cage was a ghastly sight. It had huge ears and small beady eyes set into a round flabby face. Its toothless mouth gaped open. It reminded me of the heads in the jars in Grandma's cellar.

Beezlebag was pacing up and down in front of the cages, scrutinising the baby Spriggans. He looked excited.

'I'm going to get nearer to Beezlebag to find out what he's saying,' I said.

'Be careful' replied Dill, going into crazy mode and hopping from one foot to the other. I moved closer until I could hear Beezlebag, having a conversation with Scarface.

'Look at 'em. They think they've come for a picnic. That's what they told me when I sat in on o' them crates, waiting for pop and crisps,' said Beezlebag.

'What's the plan?' asked Scarface. Beezlebag nodded towards the other Spriggans sitting round the campfire.

'Them lot are stealing the babies, then I'm supposed to go round after 'em and replace each baby they steal with one of these things, but the people who have their babies taken won't want these wretched things in their place.'

Scarface sniggered.

'Wot ye got planned for 'em?' he said.

'Me mouths watering at the thought of it,' said Beezlebag, pointing over to the Spriggans.

'They won't suspect anything cos they're as stupid as their young uns. Most of these ugly moronic brats will end up in my freezer. I'll be doing them a favour, saving 'em from the miserable loveless life I had.'

I stumbled back to Dill.

'Jaysus, Dill. That monster's only going to eat the baby Spriggans.'

'He's the devil,' said Dill hopping from one foot to another.

'They're getting ready. One of them's got earphones on and he's talking to someone on a walkie-talkie. Do something to distract him, and be quick,' I said.

Dill took a portable radio out of his pocket and tuned it to a quiet frequency. The walkie-talkie started to screech with feedback and the Spriggans gathered round the machine.

I fumbled in my bag for the bottle of midge bite lotion and whistled for Ivan, who dropped from the branch above, taking the bottle.

He scampered into the camp and emptied the contents into the large pot while the Spriggans were gathered round the screeching machine. When the machine went quiet, the Spriggans settled down to eat their broth.

'What happens now?' I whispered. Dill chuckled.

'Now we're gonna see fireworks! When they've eaten that broth, the midges will smell them from twenty miles away,' he said.

In the distance there was a rumbling, like a storm was coming. The noise grew nearer, more like a buzzing. The gloomy woods grew even gloomier, and a blackness descended on the camp. Midges were coming from every direction, millions of them, a fast-moving black cloud.

They flew down on the Spriggans, biting them all over. The Spriggans howled in pain. They flailed their arms and grabbed their bottoms, then finally they began to flee the camp, heading in different directions, some of them heading straight towards us. Dill jumped up a tree but I stood rooted to the spot, too terrified to move. One of the Spriggans ran straight into me, knocking me to the ground.

It was Beezlebag!

'It was you. I know you, you're the witch's kid. I'll get you for this,' he screamed.

He hopped up and down in an attempt to fend off the attacking hordes of midges but his screams only brought another swarm down on him and he fled, howling in pain.

After a few minutes, the camp was empty. The Spriggans had gone, leaving the babies in the cages alone. I looked at the sad, ugly baby Spriggans, and a feeling of pity for the helpless youngsters welled up inside me.

'Go and open the cages!' I shouted to Ivan, who immediately ran over and chewed the locks off each one. He shooed the babies out and they crawled off into the woods.

Dill ran over to the GPS machine and smashed it to pieces with a big stick.

I sat down on a tree stump and Dill came over to join me.

'We did it, Noola. The children of the valley are safe.'

'I'm not safe though. Did you hear Beezlebag? He said he's going to get me for this.'

As we were talking, Ivan appeared.

'That was awesome, guys.'

'Thanks, Ivan. We couldn't have done it without you,' I said.

'Well, I'm off to find the wood warden. Send out a hoot if you need me again,' he said, bounding off into the woods.

Chapter
28

A Ticket to the Fair

I need to be going. It'll take me hours to get to Bryn's house,' said Dill. I pulled my apprentice certificate and my ticket to the fair out of my pocket and handed them to him.

'I'm coming with you, Dill. I've got a ticket.'

Dill's eyes widened as he grabbed the certificate from me.

'Wow, you're an apprentice witch! Does Izzy know?'

'No, she doesn't, and it doesn't matter because I'm going to find Uncle Ned and we'll be going home.'

'But she'll be devastated, Noola. Only last week she told me how much she likes having you around.'

'She doesn't want me. She's getting rid of me as soon as the social workers can find me a home. I heard her telling Lula. Finding Uncle Ned is the only thing that keeps me getting up in the morning. Pebble Bridge isn't my home. I can't go back there anyway. Beezlebag's going to get me for this.'

Dill looked at me, a sad expression in his eyes.

'You really love your Uncle Ned, don't you?'

A lump appeared in my throat and I choked back the tears.

'He's the only person who loves me. He looked after me from being a baby; my mammy didn't want me but I think I know why now.'

'I'd go to the moon if I thought my momma was there,' said Dill, his eyes welling up. For the first time I understood why he acted so strangely.

'Oh Dill, I'm sorry. Do you remember her?'

'I remember her voice. She used to sing to me all the time. And I've got photos, but it's not the same is it?' I shook my head.

'Is your uncle a wizard or a warlock?' he asked.

'He's neither. It's Grandma's side that's magic.'

Dill looked down at the ground and spoke quietly.

'You do realise that only magic people get taken by the siseesh, don't you?'

I jumped up.

'Well, Jimmy said he could've been. And Uncle Ned had seen the fairies; he wasn't a meremortal. And besides, he told me his cousin was a right old witch.' I paced the ground in front of Dill.

'Look, are you going to take me or not?'

'Okay, come on,' he said, jumping up and pulling me along with him. 'I'm glad you're coming with me. It's going to be great fun. I'll send Zach to Poppa to tell him the Spriggans have gone and we're safe. And I'll get a message to Izzy. She's going to be so proud of you when she finds out.'

At that moment, a deep voice boomed out from above. It seemed to be coming from one of two large oak trees.

'What's all the commotion about? It woke me up,' said a face in one of the trees. I jumped up but Dill knew the tree spirit that had spoken.

'Oh, hello Filbert. We've just been seeing off a few Spriggans. Nothing to worry about. We're going to the fair on the other side of the woods.'

'Can we come?' said another face in the tree next door.

'No, it's for faery folk only,' said Dill, getting hold of my arm. 'Come on, let's go.

'Who are they?' I asked, following him.

'Filbert and Fergus,' said Dill. 'They're tree spirits. Filbert is the oldest - he's nearly a hundred and fifty years old. Fergus is much younger, about fifty, I think.' I looked back over my shoulder and couldn't believe what I saw next. First, the roots of the trees became feet, then the branches became arms with hands, and the tree spirits started to follow us.

'We might not get in,' said Filbert.

'Oh yes we will,' answered Fergus. 'There's bound to be a dodgy dwarf outside selling tickets, and if not, we'll get in through an empty tree.' I laughed. The tree spirits looked so comical, like stick insects with funny faces. I gave up resisting Dill's tugging and walked along beside him.

Chapter
29

The Fairy's Revenge

I don't know how long we'd been walking when I heard it. Somewhere in front of us a shrill spiky ringtone echoed from the trees. I stood still, unable to move. Dill crept forward and peeped round a rhododendron bush. Turning towards me he put his finger to his lips. I could hear someone talking. My heart pounded in my chest like it was trying to break straight out - I'd recognise that voice anywhere. I crept up behind Dill and peeped round the bush.

Ivan jumped from the tree above with a great deal of crackling, rustling and creaking.

'You guys didn't get far. What're ye doing here, hiding behind this bush?' he said.

'Shhh,' I pointed at Beezlebag who paced the clearing in front of us, shouting down his phone.

'What d'ya mean you're at home? Get back here this minute. We've got unfinished business with the witch's kid, and I've got to find the ingredients for the hair-restoring potion.'

A muffled voice on the other end of the phone answered before Beezlebag spoke again.

'I'm not going to eat 'er, ye dim wit. I don't want to spend the rest of mi life with 'er majesty. But accidents 'ave been known to happen, if you get my gist.'

Relief flooded through me. At least I wasn't going to suffer the same fate as the baby Spriggans.

Beezlebag sat down on a log.

'Just get 'ere fast. I'm in the clearing between Cuckoo Clough and Spooky Woods,' he said, rolling up his trousers.

Even from a distance, I could see red welts where the midges had bitten him. He pulled at a dock leaf and started frantically rubbing his leg.

Dill whispered,

'Come on, let's get out of here.'

I looked at the path littered with dead leaves and broken branches. We'd never get out of here without making a noise; he'd be sure to hear us.

At that moment, Beezlebag jumped up and looked at the log, rubbing his backside. Something seemed to have bitten him.

'Oi, yer great fat lummock. Wot d'ya fink yer doin', sittin' on us?' came a voice from the log. The log was covered in green moss, and in the moss were two twerts. He put on his glasses and peered down at them, as a tree spirit in front of him shouted, Wot d'ya think that is? I would a said it's a human but it's got a queer face.'

'Nah, that's a goblin, from the look of it. Ugly looking things those goblins. That's a goblin or I'm a fairy,' said the tree next to it. Beezlebag turned round to see who had spoken.

'See, it's a human,' said the first tree spirit.

'No, definitely goblin,' said the second.

As the trees carried on arguing, a sudden jab in his leg made Beezlebag turn around. One of the twerts had poked him with a long bony finger.

'Oi, a thought a told ye te beggar off. I'm sick o' big hairy goblins wi bums as big as prize pumpkins treating me as if a wer part o' the landscape.' Dill started to giggle.

The twert poked a moss-covered finger up its nose and pulled out a big green sticky bogey. The other twert did the same and Beezlebag stood paralysed as the twerts started to launch a barrage of bogies at him. He sat down on a clump of grass, frantically trying to pull the bogies off his face. I could see three bogies burrowing in. The first one was on his nose; he pulled that one off easily. The second was on his forehead; that, too, was struggling and he managed to pull it off. The third was on his cheek. He was just about to pull it off when the clump of grass he was sitting on jumped up, tossing him to the ground, and scampered away.

'He's gone and sat on a stray sod without realising it,' said Dill, starting to giggle uncontrollably.

'Shut up, he'll hear you,' I said.

Beezlebag staggered to the nearest tree and, checking first to make sure it didn't have a face, sat up against it. He felt his cheek, trying to find where the bogey had gone but it had disappeared. After a few minutes, he got up, staggering about and leaning on the tree to stop himself falling over. Next to the tree was a bogglestrop bush and on it something was fluttering. It looked like one of the flower fairies Dill had at home. Beezlebag reached for it and pulled off one of its wings. The fairy let out a blood-chilling scream. He dropped the fairy and put his hands over his ears to stop the terrible noise. Ivan shot up a beech tree next to the bush we were hiding behind and moments later, hundreds more of the tiny fairies appeared out of nowhere.

They swooped down on Beezlebag. Armed with tiny spears made from sharpened twigs, they attacked him from all angles. He staggered back and tripped over a rock. Falling, he banged his head on another rock and fell into the bush, knocked out cold. The fairies set to work tying him to the bush by his hair.

By now, Dill, doubled up with laughter, was hanging onto the bush for support as Ivan swung down from above us.

'Beechlings,' he said. 'You shouldn't meddle with beechlings. He won't be going anywhere for a while now.'

'Thanks, Ivan. You've saved the day again,' I said.

'Will you watch him and make sure he doesn't follow us?'

'Yes, of course, it's all part of the job. I'll be keeping him under close observation to see what he gets up to.'

'Okay, thanks. We'd better be going. We're staying over at Bryn's house tonight.'

'No problem, Noola. Always happy to help,' he said, scampering up the beech tree.

'Well, that's Beezlebag out of the way, for the time being anyway,' I said to Dill pulling him by the arm still giggling.

Chapter

30

The Journey to the Otherworld

O h, Noola. That was the funniest thing I've ever seen! I wish I'd videoed it,' Dill said, quickening his pace. He suddenly became serious, like a switch had flicked in his brain.

'Come on, we need to walk quicker; we have to get through Spooky Woods before dark.'

I clutched Dill's arm, spinning him towards me.

'You never mentioned anything about Spooky Woods before, Dill. Why is it called Spooky Woods? I don't like the sound of this.'

He started to hop up and down and his eyes became large and glassy, his expression flickering between anxiety and excitement.

'Because there are bad witches in there and maybe a few bad elves, and the trees never grow leaves. We'd better get a move on while it's still light.' He shrugged me off and headed deeper into the woods where the slowly dimming daylight glimmered through the trees. I wavered, my hand instinctively touching the St Christopher medallion round my neck. It glowed softly, reminding me why I was there. If I didn't go on, everything I had achieved up to now would be for nothing. I zipped up my coat and hurried after Dill.

Filbert and Fergus had overtaken us and were tottering in front of us like two wobbly pensioners. Filbert let out an almighty howl as he tripped over a stony twert.

'Oh, for goodness sake. Me foot's come off,' he said, hopping around the twert.

'Watch where you're going, you senile old stick insect!' it shouted.

Filbert, furious, picked up the twert and launched it towards the canal. It was about to meet a watery grave when it hit an unfortunate mallard duck who happened to be flying past. The twert hit the duck and bounced back into the woods, where a Canada goose started to peck it.

'Get off me, you feathered freak!' squealed the twert. 'Can't you see I'm not edible?'

Dill rushed over, shooed the goose away and picked up the twert, putting it into my rucksack before it knew what was happening.

'We'll take it home. Izzy's not going to be able to come to the woods for a long time,' said Dill.

Filbert was hopping about trying to put his foot back on.

'I've had enough,' he said. 'This is going to be my final journey. I'm not going back to my tree.' He hobbled along behind us with Fergus holding on to him.

As we walked a little further, the woods started to become darker and the trees looked different. Their trunks were huge and gnarled, their tortured branches covering a labyrinth of twisted, writhing roots. The trees had no leaves, despite the time of year.

'What's happening, Dill?' I asked.

'We're in Spooky Woods. Hurry up and keep going. There's all sorts of unsavoury characters in here.'

As he spoke, an elf jumped out in front of us. He was dressed in black; in fact, everything about him was black. His cold dark eyes, sunk deep into his head, glittered like shards of granite.

'Who's this then?' he said. 'Well, if it isn't one of the Cobnutts. I thought you lot were long gone from these parts. What are you doing in my woods?'

Dill squared up to the elf.

'Let us pass. We're going to the fair. We don't want any trouble.'

The elf blocked our path, his scowl turning into a leer.

'Well then, my little pixie, what's in the bag?'

Without warning, he stuck his hand into my bag and let out a howl of pain. The stony twert had bitten him and was now dangling from his finger as he jumped up and down in agony.

Dill pulled me past the black elf who whirled his hand above his head, trying to remove the furious twert. The twert let go and went flying past me, landing amongst a clump of ferns.

'Come on, quickly,' said Dill. We need to get to Bryn's house before it gets dark.' I turned round to see the black elf still jumping up and down and hurried after Dill.

As we walked, the light was fading, casting sinister shadows amongst the trees.

Dill moved easily, accustomed to being outside in the dark, but I could barely see a thing. I was trying not to trip up when I felt a sharp nip on my ankle. Looking down, I saw something about the size of a small black dog without a tail staring up at me.

I screamed, which evidently wasn't the correct thing to do, because now about a dozen of the black creatures with vicious eyes appeared out of the slowly dimming light and started to nip our ankles.

Dill jumped up the nearest tree, pulling me up behind him.

'They're blind mimps,' he shouted above the racket of the mimps, who were now howling like a pack of bloodthirsty hounds at the bottom of the tree.

I looked down and immediately wished I hadn't. Although they had the bodies of animals, their features were almost human. They had long beaky noses which they held up to the air trying to identify the whereabouts of their prey. Their eyes, however, were the most hideous thing about them: no pupils, just huge bulging whites. Dill climbed higher up the

tree, pulling me behind him. Reaching the top, we found a large branch and stopped to catch our breath.

'What do we do now? I'm not going back down there, but we can't stop here,' I said. Dill reached into his jacket pocket and pulled out a bottle. It was bogglestrop juice.

'Is it enough to get us away from here?' I asked.

'Enough to get us home and back. I made it super concentrated,' he said with a manic glint in his eyes. He took a huge gulp before passing it to me.

'Take a drink, then watch me and do what I do.'

I hesitated. I'd seen the effect it had on people but if it meant getting away from the mimps... I took a small sip. It tasted surprisingly pleasant.

'Right, we need to wait about five minutes then put your arms straight up and head upwards,' said Dill.

After a few minutes, I began to feel strange. My stomach started to swell, getting bigger and bigger. Dill's stomach was swelling, too.

He lifted one arm into the air and grabbed my hand with his other hand. He quickly floated upwards, taking me with him. 'Don't look down!' he shouted as we drifted across the treetops.

After about five minutes, the trees started to thin out and a clearing appeared below. Dill shouted,

'Burp, Noola, burp!' We both started to burp, letting the air out of our stomachs. Gradually we dropped and landed on the soft grass a short distance away. We'd escaped!

The moon shone brightly, lighting up the clearing.

'I'm glad you're with me and not Izzy,' said Dill. 'She'd have just zapped those mimps with her magic wand, but that was much more fun.'

'Grandma's got a magic wand?' I said incredulously.

'Of course she has. She's a witch, isn't she. She rarely uses it, though, just in emergencies. You'll get one when you're fully qualified.'

'Wow! It'd be fun to have a magic wand,' I said. 'I wish I'd had one when I was getting picked on at school.'

The snap of a branch and rustling amongst the undergrowth finished our conversation and I took hold of Dill's arm.

'Come on, let's get out of here. I hope there's no more nasty surprises. I just want to get to the fair in one piece.'

The night was warm and balmy and we soon reached Bryn's house.

Bryn lived with his friend, Rodger, and together they ran a guest house called Bodgers, which was surprisingly grand by elf standards. It was three storeys high and decorated with colourful window boxes full of marigolds and geraniums. Outside was a patio area with a pergola draped with bunting and lit up with fairy lights. A wonderful smell wafted from a barbecue where a bald-headed elf was turning over sausages and singing opera at the top of his voice.

Bryn spotted Dill and put down his tongs.

'Dill, daaahling, it's wonderful to see you!' he said, flinging his arms round Dill and hugging him. Dill stood still, looking slightly bemused.

'Isabel broke her leg, so I'm taking Noola to the fair. This is Isabel's granddaughter.'

'Wellll, little pixie,' Bryn grabbed my hand, clasping it tightly, 'I'm very pleased to meet you. Would you like a hot dog with my special beechnut and nettle sausage?'

'Thanks,' I said, 'I'd love one. I'm starving.'

Bryn pulled out two seats at a table and resumed his cooking.

'Looks like you're pretty full,' said Dill.

'Yes, Ostara Fair. Always booked up this week of the year. We have two elves from London. That's them over there, Eddie and Philip, or Pip, as he prefers to be called.'

The two elves from London looked up and one of them smiled and waved.

'That's Eddie,' said Bryn. 'Quite trendy, isn't he?'

Eddie was dressed in a rainbow-coloured suit.

'He isn't like any elf I've ever seen,' said Dill, picking a sausage off the grill. Pip looked just as colourful in a purple tie-dyed vest and yellow leggings.

'They're from Hackney,' said Bryn.

'The other guests are from Scotland. Strange ones, mind you. That's them up there.' He pointed up into the sky, where, sure enough, six elves were floating above us in earnest conversation, dressed in the Scottish national costume.

'They've had too much bogglestrop and burdock soda, but I suppose they'll come down when they're hungry. You can have Isabel's room, Noola, and you can sleep in the attic, Dill,' said Bryn.

'How's Rodger?' asked Dill through a mouth full of sausage.

'He's wonderful,' replied Bryn.' He's in the kitchen baking pavlova. It's the best pavlova in the whole of elfdom.'

As he was speaking, a short, stout little elf in a flowery pinafore emerged from a green door. Spotting Dill, he threw his arms round him.

'Dill, my little cutie, how are you? And look, you've found yourself a girlfriend at last.'

Dill blushed. 'Oh no, she's not my girlfriend. She's Isabel's granddaughter. We're going to the fair.'

'Of course, it is. I see the resemblance to Pixie,' said Rodger. 'Pleased to meet you, missy. How's that cheeky grandad of yours?'

'Oh, I haven't met him yet. I'm hoping he'll be at the fair,' I replied.

'Oh, he might be, with that clever parrot of his no doubt. I heard he was back up north,' said Rodger.

Bryn shot him a pointed look and passed me a hot dog.

'Yes, and dragging that poor family of his behind him. It's time he stopped traipsing round the countryside and settled down. Those youngsters of his need to go to school.' Bryn looked at me.

'Sorry, Noola, but I don't much care for your grandad.'

I thought back to all the arguments between Uncle Ned and Mammy about her not sending me to school. Grandad was doing the same thing to his kids, and he'd stolen Juno.

My face burned and I looked at my feet. I was so mad with Grandad, I'd suddenly lost my appetite.

Rodger saw the look of dismay on my face. 'Here, have one of these,' he said, handing me a sticky bun.

As I sat looking at the bun in one hand and the hot dog in the other, my mind was on tomorrow. First, I'd find Uncle Ned, then we'd decide what to do about Grandad.

I lay in bed trying to sleep. A light tapping on the window interrupted my thoughts and I slipped out of bed, opening the window wide enough to hear an owl hooting in the distance and a branch creaking above my head.

I looked up to see Ivan swinging to and fro from the branch, waving a stick around. I opened the window wide enough for him to jump inside. Somehow, I knew he hadn't come with good news.

'What's happened? What're you doing here?' I asked.

'Beezlebag's on the loose again. Scarface came for him. It was funny really. Dill would've wet himself.'

'Why, what happened?'

'Beezlebag woke up just after you left. He must have been hungry because he started to eat the bogglestrop berries. He blew up like a balloon and was floating in the air. He was still bleeding and was black and blue from his encounter with the fairies, and he was still attached to the bush by his hair.'

'What happened then?' I asked.

'Scarface set to work, hacking his hair to free him.

When he cut the last bit that was tethering him to the bush, there was a tremendous whoosh and Beezlebag set off like a rocket. He slammed from one tree to another until he landed with a smack at the base of a large oak tree. He looked like he'd been in a horrific car accident. He must be made of strong stuff coz after a few minutes he got up. He was talking to Scarface and they set off into the woods. I thought I'd better come and let you know.'

'Well, he probably won't make it to the fair tomorrow and even if he does, Uncle Ned will be there. I'm not worried about him. Uncle Ned will protect me. But thanks anyway.'

'Okay, Noola. I'm off home now. It's been a very tiring day.'

With that, Ivan jumped onto the window ledge and with a flying leap was back in the tree and scampering away.

I had trouble falling asleep after Ivan had gone. I thought of Uncle Ned. He was twice the size of Beezlebag and in a fight there'd be no contest. But as I listened to the wind whistling through the trees, I wondered why I felt so scared.

Chapter
31

Ostara Fair

I woke up to the sun shining and a cloudless sky. The brightness of the day lifted my mood and I felt hopeful. Rodger waved us off. He'd packed us a picnic of sausage rolls, herb bread and blackcurrant jam. We stopped at a place called Dingle Dell and ate our picnic in a little clearing with the sun streaming through the trees.

After walking for another hour, a feeling of déjà vu washed over me. Somewhere up ahead I could hear children's laughter, the same sound I'd heard during the siseesh.

I stood perfectly still, my breathing fast and shallow. In front of us, thousands of fireflies illuminated a path which led to a gap in the trees.

'We're here,' said Dill, pulling me forward.

Once we were through the trees, an eerie mist descended upon us making it difficult to see so we headed towards the noise. The sound of laughter grew louder and as the mist cleared, I could make out a gate guarded by dwarfs who all had large pot bellies, short stumpy legs and straggly dreadlocks. Their round, surly faces scowled at the elves, witches and goblins coming at them from all directions.

As we waited in the queue, I could hear the shouting and laughter of hundreds of people beyond the fence mixed with organ music from the fairground rides.

Dill started to bounce up and down as I produced the tickets from my pocket and handed them to one of the dwarfs. The dwarf looked at me from beneath his bushy eyebrows.

'You're a bit young for a witch's apprentice, aren't ye? And wot's up with Tigger, here? As e' bin on the loopy juice? If he carries on like that he won't be in there long he'll get slung out.'

I held on to Dill's arm to stop him bouncing.

'He's just a bit excitable, that's all and I'm a newly qualified witch, last week actually,' I said.

'Well, bring some ID next time,' said the surly dwarf, tearing the tickets in two and stamping our hands.

We walked through the huge gates. The posts were made from three thorn trees intertwined. Two owls sat on the gate posts, one on either side. As we walked past, the owls' heads rotated, but their bodies remained still. All my senses were heightened. All the colours seemed brighter. I started to tremble… I was entering the Otherworld.

As we passed through the gates, I gasped. In front of us was a huge mountain with a waterfall running through the middle of it and a sign saying **LOG FLUME**. Young elves were sitting astride logs, flying down the flowing water and howling with excitement. The waterfall flowed into a lake with a large, grassed area in front of it - marquees on one side and picnic tables on the other. Down the side of the picnic tables were carts with all sorts of delicious smells coming from them.

When I had lived in Ireland, Uncle Ned had taken me to the fair in Ballybay every year, but that fair was nothing like this one. Here, there were rollercoasters and dodgems, helter-skelters and merry-go-rounds, but none of them seemed to be powered by generators; there wasn't a cable to be seen.

In the middle of the fair was a merry-go-round, a huge oak tree with hammocks tied to its branches. Dill started to run towards it.

'Come on, Noola. Let's have a go on it.'

I didn't want to go on the rides. I was going to look for Uncle Ned, and besides, at the fair in Ballybay, the rides just made me sick.

'No, Dill, you go. I'll come and find you later. I'm going to look for Uncle Ned.' I felt suddenly empty. If he was here, surely I'd know - I'd sense it. It frightened me that I didn't.

I shut my eyes tightly, took some deep breaths and opened them. He had to be here.

I walked over to one of the marquees. It had a sign outside saying **TWERTS - THREE FOR THE PRICE OF TWO.**

I went inside, scanning the crowds, but all I could see were witches and goblins. I felt numb, detached, as if my body was getting on with life, as if it mattered. If I couldn't find Uncle Ned, nothing mattered. Nothing would matter ever again.

The marquee was hot and stuffy. There were hundreds of tables with cages on them and inside the cages were the twerts, strange-looking creatures of every conceivable shape and size. The noise was deafening.

I walked down the first aisle, hypnotised by the creatures in the cages. I stopped to look at one with a sign saying **STONY TWERT – POMPOUS.**

The twert puffed out its chest and spoke.

'Stop looking at me, you ignorant small person. Stop looking at me or I'll vomit all over you.'

I moved on to the next cage. This twert had a label saying **CUNNING TWERT**. It smiled sweetly at me.

'Come closer, dear,' it said. 'Let me look at your beautiful green eyes.' I drew nearer, putting my face up close to the cage. The twert stuck a long bony finger through the bars and poked me in the eye.

'Take that, you freak,' it said.

I jumped back in pain, my eyes watering but carried on.

As I strolled down the aisles, the marquee seemed to be emptying. I looked around to find out why when a tap on my shoulder made me jump. Standing behind me was Juli Anabaluloo. She looked majestic in a blue and gold kaftan with a matching turban.

'Hi, Noola. I wondered if you'd be here. Did you find your uncle?' she said, squeezing my shoulder.

'Er, well, I've just arrived and started looking but he's not in here.'

'Where's your grandma?'

'Grandma's broken her leg so I have to help Dill with the shopping but he's gone to the fair.'

'Well, I can't find your uncle but I can help you with the shopping. Do you have a list?'

I passed Juli the shopping list and she reached into her hold-all, put on a pair of gold-rimmed glasses and read it out.

Stony twerts 8
(2 cunning, 2 pompous, 2 cantankerous, 2 addictive)
Mossy twerts 10
(2 lazy, 2 greedy, 2 simpering, 1 ignorant,
1 sullen, 2 vain)
Fungal twerts
(4 anything they have)

'Hmm looks like she need mostly mossy.'

She led me down the aisles of noisy twerts who were
shouting abuse at one another and at anyone who came near
them. Each one had a label giving its name and uses.

'These here are the mossy ones. They're used for affecting
potions. They change the way people act or feel, and they can
cure lots of ailments. That one there is a greedy one. Deadly
bogies, they have,' said Juli.

The cages of the mossy twerts were made of glass with air
holes in the top. The glass was covered in wriggling slimy things.

All the twerts had long thin arms and long fingers. They
didn't have legs, so they couldn't run away, but they had very
human faces… and temperaments.

We carried on to the next aisle.

'These here are the stony ones, best for transforming
potions, and them over there are the fungal ones. I ain't
going near them. They make me cough uncontrollably,' Juli
explained.

'Could I ask you,' I said, 'why there aren't any good twerts?'

'Because good people don't come back as twerts.'

'What happens to them, then?' I asked, thinking of Uncle
Ned.

'Well, that depends on lots of things. If you're religious
or atheist or if you're one of us.' Look, it's complicated and I
haven't got the time to go into it.'

I wasn't satisfied.

'Please, I need to know,' I said, my voice sounding thick and strange. Juli sighed.

'Some religions believe you go to heaven, and some believe you come back to the earth to a better life. Why do you ask?' Her eyes grew large as she stared deep into my eyes and she seemed to read my mind. I looked down, unable to speak as a tear sneaked out of the corner of my eye. She spoke softly.

'When you lose someone you love, they become a star, shining down on you and looking after you, like a guardian angel. They don't leave you,' she said. I touched the St Christopher round my neck. Juli carried on.

'If you're not religious, you come back as a spirit reflected in the beauty of nature, usually a tree or a bird.'

Turning things over in my mind, I had stopped listening. Juli nudged me.

'So, the moral of the story is, be good or be a witch!

I wouldn't fancy coming back as a twert. Now come on, let's get this shopping list of yours sorted.'

We walked back to the stall selling mossy twerts.

'Oi, Blodwyn,' Juli shouted to a rather grumpy-looking dwarf. 'Take this order for Isabel Flynn. We haven't got all day.' The dwarf shuffled over and took the list from Juli.

'Deliver it, please. The child can't carry this lot, and don't be putting in any mouldy ones. She wants the freshest you have.'

'Thanks very much,' I said to the dwarf. 'My grandma will pay you when you bring them, and thanks Juli.'

'Now, you go out an' have some fun on them rides and be sure to get home before dark. There's mischief an' evil around and you'd do well to avoid it.' With that, she strode away.

I wanted to double check Uncle Ned wasn't there so I carried on looking. The twerts in Grandma's cellar were scary but seeing so many in one place was beginning to freak me out.

I carried on down an aisle, following a sign FUNGAL TWERTS.

In the first cage, something resembling a huge mushroom was rolling about in some straw. It opened one of its eyes and started to speak.

'I have a terrible itch, a most annoying itch on my back. Would you scratch it for me, please?' it said, in a deep croaky voice. The twert turned round to reveal a very hairy back. As I put my hand into the cage and scratched it, great clouds of stinking smoke started oozing out of the twert's back, making me cough and sneeze. The smoke fumes started to fill the marquee, causing everyone else to cough and sneeze as well.

Too late, I noticed a sign straight in front of me. In bold black capital letters, it said: DO NOT TOUCH THE TWERTS.

I quickly left the marquee and went into the next one, hoping no one had seen me.

This tent was the same as the last one - full of witches, apart from goblins selling their wares.

It was hopeless. I was about to go back outside when I saw a witch with the same cloak as Grandma and I felt a pang of remorse. Grandma was in hospital because of me. The least I could do for her was get her shopping. Dill was too busy having fun to do it, and besides, when I found Uncle Ned, getting the shopping was the last thing I'd want to be doing. I turned around.

Inside, the marquee was packed. Witches of all shapes and sizes jostled each other to get to the front where a long table was piled up with baskets full of weird and wacky things. I squirmed my way through, ducking under arms and in between legs until I reached the front.

I squeezed between the other witches, scanning the faces. I read the shopping list: blind worm's sting, lizard's eyeballs, dragon's teeth. This list seemed a bit more straightforward. I stood holding it as high as I could before realising it was hopeless. I wished I was taller. The goblins who were serving were just ignoring me.

All of a sudden, the jabbering stopped followed by a
hushed silence as one by one the witches around me started
to drift away. I turned round to see what was happening and
saw Juli again.

'You still shopping?'

'Yes. I've got a few more things to get,' I said.

The only ones left in the marquee now were the goblins
serving behind the counter. They were gathered in a group,
cowering in a corner. Juli shouted to one of them. 'Hey, curly
beard, come serve this child. She's been waiting ages.'

'What's wrong with them?' I asked as the goblin came over.
They looked visibly shaken but too scared to disobey Juli.

'Oh. they're scared of me. I just turned one of them in the
last marquee into a goat. He was actin' like a silly old goat, so
I turned him into one.'

I gasped.

'Don't worry, child, I'll turn him back before I go.'

The goblin served me straightaway. 'Throw some o' them
screech owl claws in for free, an' a few hares' whiskers,' Juli

shouted to the goblin, who could hardly hold the bag as he was trembling so much.

'An' put it down for delivering to Isabel Flynn, Pebble Bridge. An' she wants it this week.' She turned to me.

'By the way, how did you get on with my necklace?'

I told her the story of Ivan the Muscovy and the Spriggans. Juli laughed her deep throaty laugh.

'I told you you was gonna need it one day.' She put her hand on my shoulder.

'If you ever want a change of scene, you can come work for me anytime.' She winked at me as she walked away.

'Thanks, Juli,' I said as she left the marquee and went outside.

Chapter
32

Pixie Flynn

The fair was heaving by this time. I wandered around, passing the same stalls more than once, searching everywhere. As I pushed my way through the crowds, getting jostled and bumped, I smelled a familiar smell. Two goblins were in front of me, one of them drinking from a bottle. He seemed to be staggering, his speech slurred.

'This stuff's unbelievable. It's got the kick of a mule,' he said.

I started to tremble. *It was the smell of moonshine.*

'Where'd ya get it from?' asked the second goblin.

'Back o' that bow-top over there. There's an Irish fella selling it,' replied the tipsy goblin.

In the distance I spotted a colourful bow-top caravan. It was a proper old-fashioned gypsy caravan, beautifully painted in green, white and gold. At the back of the caravan was a cart piled high with crates. Someone was handing over bottles from the crates and taking money.

I ran towards it. 'Please let it be Uncle Ned, please,' I whispered.

When I got nearer, the figure came into focus. I stopped abruptly. The face seemed familiar but it wasn't Uncle Ned. It was a teenage boy standing on the back of the cart selling the whiskey.

I stood perfectly still. Uncle Ned was nowhere to be seen.

My blood turned to ice and I became terribly cold. For a moment, I was back in Ballybay at the top of a steep cliff, looking down. I could feel the rush of the wind on my face; I could taste the salty spray of the sea. I started to fall. I was hurtling down the cliff, heading for the crashing waves at the bottom. I wanted to feel the sea, for it to be over. I wanted to be with Uncle Ned.

Staggering round to the other side of the cart I felt the ground coming towards me. I grabbed hold of the cart and fell to my knees.

Curling up into a ball, I held my face in my hands and started to cry. I cried more than I had ever cried before, even more than I had after he had disappeared. Great heaving sobs.

I replayed the events of that terrible day in my mind. I saw Uncle Ned's face as he lay motionless on the sand and I knew he wasn't here. He was never going to be here. Maybe I'd known it from the beginning.

I sat for what seemed like hours, my body chilled and numb, even though it was a warm spring day. My mind drifted back to the night before he'd disappeared. I still couldn't force myself to say the other word.

His words came back to me again. They sounded distant, like when I used to listen to the sound of the sea in a shell.

'Even when I'm not around, I'll still be with you. I'll always be with you.'

Now I realised, he'd known. In his own way, he'd been trying to tell me, and now, I knew.

Eventually, I felt the St Christopher round my neck begin to warm me. I thought back to all the times I'd been truly afraid, or really sad, when the medallion had comforted me. And that's when I understood. *He was here* - I felt his presence. *He was still here.* The warmth started to seep into my arms and legs and the feeling in them returned. I could hear voices. At first, they seemed to be coming from far away but they grew louder until I realised they were coming from the caravan in front of the cart.

I slowly got to my feet, dried my eyes and joined the crowd of people gathered round the bow-top.

On a bench at the front of the caravan, a man was shouting.

'Go on, ask him. Ask him anything,' he said to the crowd. In his hand was a bottle and he took a swig of it every now and again.

'What's the capital of France?' shouted a young elf at the front of the crowd.

A beautiful yellow blue and red parrot hopped on to the man's outstretched arm. The parrot couldn't fly away; it was tethered by a short chain to the bench. The man looked too familiar - he was an older, male version of me. It could only be my grandad, Pixie Flynn - and on his arm was Juno!

'Paris, monsieur, Paris,' said Juno. Everyone in the audience whistled and cheered.

'What's one hundred and eighty-seven, and three hundred and fifty-two?' shouted someone else.

Juno cocked her head to one side. 'Five hundred and thirty-nine, most definitely,' she said. The crowd went wild.

Grandad jumped down
from the caravan and
walked round the crowd
who were so impressed by
the parrot that the hat was
soon filled with coins.

He jumped back up, on
a roll now. 'Go on, ask it
some…

At that moment, his
eyes met mine. He stopped
shouting and dropped
the bottle he was holding,
which smashed as it hit the
ground, startling the crowd.

His eyes grew wide.

The crowd grew silent as everyone turned to look at me.

'Hello, Grandad. I'm Noola, Bridget's daughter.'

He jumped off the wagon and lifted me up into the air.

'Well, would ya believe it! I didn't even know I had a
granddaughter, but here she is as large as life in front of me.'

One by one, the crowd drifted away.

'Come and meet your family,' he said, putting me down
onto the bow-top and hopping up after me.

We went inside the caravan, which reminded me of
Grandma's front room.

It was warm and cosy with a small wood-burning stove
in the corner. There wasn't much furniture; the family
were sitting on cushions on the floor. They were watching
television and didn't seem too impressed that their
programme had been interrupted. There were three small
boys, a wood elf feeding a baby and one other girl about the
same age and size as me.

The family gaped in amazement at me. I was, as everyone had told me, the spitting image of my grandad.

'This is Noola, everyone. She's the daughter of my eldest daughter, Bridget. Where is Bridget, by the way?' said Grandad, turning towards me.

'Is she with you?'

'No, she went to London. I'm staying with Grandma,' I answered.

'She's not here, is she?' asked Grandad, the smile disappearing off his face.

'No, she's broken her leg,' I replied.

He let out a sigh of relief.

I suddenly remembered my manners.

'Pleased to meet you all,' I said, and I was – sort of. But I felt empty. The hope I'd had this morning had gone, and I didn't feel like being sociable.

The tallest girl stood up, her eyes wide in the gloom. She could have been my twin, apart from the colour of her hair which was blonde and her eyes which were blue. She had the same freckles that I used to have, which made her face look muddy. We were different shades of the same image.

She eyed me warily. I stared back.

'Where's your manners, Olive. Take the baby while your mother makes Noola some tea,' said Grandad.

The girl took the baby from her mother, sticking the bottle roughly into its mouth.

'Move up and let her sit down. We were just about to have tea, weren't we, Maggie?' said Grandad. Maggie frowned at me, her face sullen. Her eyes were large and dark, but with no gentleness in them. She disappeared through a curtain at the front of the caravan.

The tallest boy spoke.

'Daddy, can we go to the fair this afternoon?'

'No, you can't Kiernan,' said Grandad. 'Go take Billy and help Caelan with the whiskey, then you can chop some wood for the fire.'

'Olive, put the baby in its crib, and go help your mother with the tea.'

The man's a tyrant, I thought, as he went back outside, leaving us alone. Olive disappeared behind a small curtain and came back with a tray. On it was a teapot some cups and a plate piled high with fruit cake.

'Do you go to school?' She asked, handing me a cup of tea. I've just started. How about you?'

'Never been. We travel round the country going to fairs. It's how we earn our money. With the parrot and from selling moonshine.'

'What's it like?' she said, passing me a plate filled with cake. 'What's what like?' I asked.

'School.' I took a bite of cake and thought about it.

'Overrated, and there's bullies,' I said.

'One day,' Olive said, 'we'll settle down, and we'll buy a big house with a river at the bottom of it and we'll have servants and a big car, and then we'll be able to go to school.'

Grandad is making a fortune out of Juno, I thought.

After I had eaten two pieces of fruit cake and drank two cups of tea, I got up to leave. 'I'll have to be going now,' I said.

'Yes, fine, you go. It's getting late. Pixie will be finished soon,' said Maggie, smiling for the first time since I arrived.

When I went outside. The crowds were gone and Grandad was fast asleep in an armchair, snoring loudly with a half-drunk bottle of whiskey beside him.

On his belt was a large ring with a single key. Juno eyed me warily as I unhooked the key and unlocked the padlock attached to her leg. I replaced the key, but Juno didn't move. Not until I whispered in her ear,

'Fly away, Juno. Go find Jonjo.'

Juno cocked her head, then took off into the sky. I decided I'd better leave quickly before Grandad woke up. I jumped off the bow top and disappeared into the crowd to look for Dill. The night was drawing in and soon it would be dark.

I headed for the fairground rides and found him being catapulted into the sky on a ride called the Elf Slinger.

He soared through the sky and landed a hundred metres away on a rubber mattress. I ran over and helped him up.

'Did you find your uncle?' he asked.

I looked up at the sky and blinked away my tears.

Dill spoke quietly. 'I pretended Momma was coming back for years. It's not weird, it's a normal reaction. You believe a comforting lie because the truth is so hard to take.'

'How did you get over it, Dill?' I asked, touching the medallion round my neck.

'I had a good family. Doesn't sound like the same can be said of yours.'

He put his arm round my shoulders. 'But you've got Izzy and you've got me and Poppa. We'll be your family now.'

From the other side of the field, a tannoy announced the fireworks display was about to start. Dill grabbed my arm, pulling me behind him.

'Come on, let's go see the fireworks,' he said, pushing through the crowd. 'We'll get to the front to get a good view.'

We got to the front just as the display was about to start.

An elf was running round with a taper. He lit the fuse of a huge rocket.

Dill suddenly jumped up. He grabbed hold of my arm, trying to drag me out of the way. Everyone started to scream and there was mass panic as people tried to flee.

The elf was Beezlebag and he was aiming the rocket straight at me.

Dill screamed, 'Run, Noola, run!'

I wanted to run but my legs wouldn't move. I felt a sudden warmth from the St Christopher round my neck. There was a rustling noise and a mini tornado appeared in the distance, swirling up little clouds of dust. It was accompanied by the same eerie whistling sound I had heard twice before - the sound of the siseesh.

The bunting around the firework display started to spin wildly, as if someone had pressed the button on a fruit machine.

Filbert and Fergus had come to watch the display and were standing just to the side of the rocket. The taper was lit now and pointing towards me and the fleeing crowd. When Filbert realised what was happening he grabbed Beezlebag by the collar and strode across to the rocket, pointing it towards the sky.

Then with a whoosh, it was off. Filbert clung on, one long branch-like arm holding on to the rocket and the other clinging on to Beezlebag, who was kicking and screaming, his arms and legs flailing in panic. When the rocket had

climbed high into the
sky there was a massive
explosion and the sky lit
up with a bang. The air
was filled with thousands
of glittering sparks thrown
like diamonds into the
night, followed by plumes
of vibrant blue, red and
purple smoke ribboning
into the sky before fading
to a ghostly grey, clouding
out the stars.

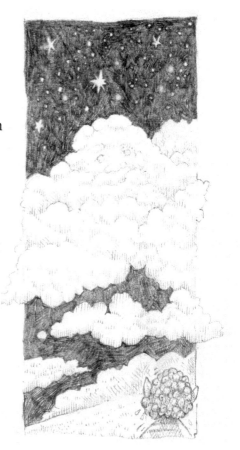

I stood transfixed.
There, in the smoke, I
saw the face of Uncle
Ned smiling down on
me. I was still shaking
as I watched the smoke
disappear, leaving a star-
filled sky.

Tears started to trickle
down my face.

One star looked particularly bright.

'Thanks Uncle Ned,' I whispered.

All around me people were panicking and I was pushed
around by the frightened crowds.

Dill came back to find me. I was standing exactly where he
had left me.

'That was stupid, Noola. You could have been killed. Why
didn't you run?'

I still felt peculiarly calm.

'It's okay, Dill. Someone was looking after me.'

I felt as if I was somewhere else, floating, looking down at the chaos around me. It was as if a heavy weight had been lifted off my shoulders; the pain I'd carried round these last few months had disappeared.

From the other side of the fairground came an almighty scream, jolting me out of my thoughts. Someone was yelling, cursing and swearing.

Everyone was looking to see what the commotion was about, but I knew: the fireworks must have woken Grandad and he had found Juno gone.

'Quick, Dill, we need to get out of here. I've released Juno and it looks like Grandad's found out. He sounds pretty mad. We need to be quick, but the gate's miles away. Is there another way?'

Dill's eyes lit up.

'Yes. Come on, follow me.'

The yelling was getting closer and I could see Grandad approaching in the distance. I ran after Dill who was heading for the Elf Slinger. We jumped over the barrier. The ride was closed for the day, but Dill knew exactly what to do - he had spent most of the day on it.

'Quick, put this on.' He handed me a parachute and put one on himself. I felt sick, but it was the only way. Grandad had spotted us and was running now.

Dill fiddled with the controls, changing the speed to fifty kilometres per hour and the distance to two kilometres. We jumped into the sling together and within seconds, we were flying through the air.

We must have been travelling for about a minute when Dill shouted,

'Pull the cord, Noola!'

He'd noticed the trees thinning out and worked out we must be near Bryn's house. We both pulled the red cords and the parachutes opened, pulling us high into the air and

back towards the trees. I threw up. I couldn't see where we were, but I could hear Dill's hysterical laughter. Gradually, we floated downwards, our parachutes tangled in the trees, but we'd done it – we'd escaped.

Dill managed to untangle himself and came to free me.

We walked for a little while until we arrived at Bodgers, where Bryn welcomed us. After a supper of buttered crumpets with honey, we both went to bed, exhausted.

I looked out of the window and took one last look at the bright star twinkling above. 'Goodnight, Uncle Ned,' I said.

Chapter

33

Home

The journey back through Spooky Woods was unadventurous. In the cold light of day, there was nothing spooky about them. As we walked along, I noticed Fergus trudging wearily back to his tree. I ran to catch up with him.

'Hi, Fergus. I'm sorry about Filbert. What he did was unbelievably brave,' I said.

'Oh, don't be sorry about it,' said Fergus. 'Filbert was a very old oak tree. He'd had thousands of acorns. Scattered everywhere, they are. He'd done his bit for humanity.

'Do you know, in his lifetime he'd produced 39,000 pounds of oxygen.

'Lately, though, he'd become very disenchanted. The whispering winds have told us that in other countries humans are slaughtering trees in their thousands. Deforestation they call it. It made Filbert very angry.'

'Yes, I've heard about that; our tree spirit Buddy told me. Humans can be incredibly stupid, can't they?'

'Yes, incredibly. But you know, Filbert had always wanted to fly. He was envious of the birds. So you see, he was happy to go that way. Life's a cycle and his life was over. He was very brittle, always losing his branches. And you must admit, he did go out with a bang.' Filbert giggled.

'I've still got my memories. We had some great laughs.'

I thought back to Ballybay and what Jimmy had said: Don't be sad for what you've lost, be happy for what you had. For the first time since Uncle Ned had gone, I remembered him and smiled.

We arrived back in Pebble Bridge in the afternoon. I left Dill and headed home. As I approached Grandma's house, I saw a crowd of people outside. When they saw me, they began to cheer and clap. Katy and her mum were at the front of the crowd with Erin. Katy rushed towards me. 'Thank you, Noola. Fred told us what you did and we'll never forget it. I'm sorry for being so mean. I promise I'll never fall out with you again,' she said, throwing her arms round me.

I noticed Fred in the cheering crowd. He was smiling and waving, too. I hugged Katy back and went over to him.

'What you did was awesome. Gobbit's never gonna be able to touch you again after this. You're a hero,' he said.

The crowd gathered round me and the next moment I found myself being hugged by everyone.

Grandma came out of the house. She was on crutches and her face gave away either pain or anger. I was unsure which. She looked frail and vulnerable and my heart ached at the thought that I had caused it. She half smiled and I followed her into the house.

She sighed.

'It's okay, Noola. I know what happened. I'd like to have met your Uncle Ned. It sounds like he was quite a character.'

'How did you find out?' I said, choking back the tears.

'Dill rang Sorrel and told him the whole story. I'd guessed a lot of it anyway. I knew something was going on, and when I arrived home from hospital there was a letter from the witches' council telling me what a great apprentice you are.'

'I'm sorry, Grandma. I didn't like all the sneaking about but I heard you telling Lula you were sending me to a foster home.'

'So, you imagined your uncle was still alive and that he'd be at the fair, and the only way you could get a ticket was to become an apprentice witch.'

'Yes, something like that, but I really believed he'd be there. You must think I'm really stupid.'

'I don't think you're stupid. It's a normal reaction when a child loses someone they love. They pretend it isn't happening and live in a fantasyland where the person is coming back.'

'I'm sorry, Grandma,' I said again.

A trace of a smile flickered across her face.

'I'm sorry, too. I shouldn't have reacted the way I did when you turned up, its not your fault your parents are feckless and irresponsible. I should have realised you were different from your Mammy.' She held out her arms and I hugged her tight.

'I was frightened I'd lose you too.' She pulled back and smiled. A happy smile this time.

'Come on, I've got a surprise for you.'

I followed her into the room where there were balloons and a table filled with sandwiches, cakes and buns, and in the cage next to Jonjo was Juno. They were pecking and preening each other.

'Welcome home,' said Grandma. 'It's your home now for as long as you want to stay here, and I'd like you to be my official apprentice. You're going to make a great witch.'

A flood of relief and happiness rushed through me.

'Thanks, Grandma,' I said. 'And I promise, I'll never hide anything from you ever again.'

Everyone crowded into the little cottage and the party went on all day.

Sorrel had told everyone about how me and Dill had got rid of the Spriggans and the news had spread around the town.

That night, before I went to bed, I got out my notebook.

I picked up my pen.

Find Juno. I ticked it.
Be a hedgewitch, like Grandma. I ticked it.
And finally, Find Uncle Ned.

I went to the window. The star was still there. It was the brightest in the sky and shining straight down on me.
I went back to my notebook and ticked it.

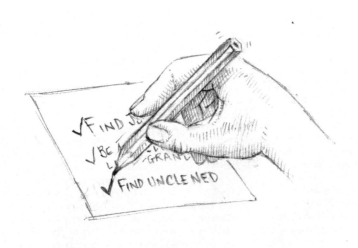

Lightning Source UK Ltd.
Milton Keynes UK
UKHW011827191121
394181UK00002B/24